CUT AND SHOOT

Suddenly Bell felt the mustang's muscles tighten and saw its ears come up.

He drew up, listening. A moment passed and then he smelled woodsmoke and heard voices . . . the voices of Devitt's men.

Inside him something welled up and burst.

He dropped his hand to his gun and he yelled, a wild rebel yell torn with pain and fury. And then he slapped spurs to the horse and leaped him through the brush into the firelight.

Startled lumberjacks came to their feet, eyes wild.

One man grabbed at a rifle, but Bell's gun smashed a shot and the man screamed, dropping the rifle to grab a broken shoulder. A bullet smashed the coffee pot, another ripped at the bed of the fire, scattering sparks and embers.

Then he was across the camp and gone into darkness, his gun stabbing flame.

BRIONNE
THE BROKEN GUN
THE BURNING HILLS
THE CALIFORNIOS
CALLAGHEN
CATLOW
CHANCY
CONAGHER
DARK CANYON
THE DAYBREAKERS
DOWN THE LONG HILLS
THE EMPTY LAND
FALLON
THE FERGUSON RIFLE
THE FIRST FAST DRAW
FLINT
GALLOWAY
GUNS OF THE TIMBERLANDS
HANGING WOMAN CREEK
THE HIGH GRADERS
HIGH LONESOME
HOW THE WEST WAS WON
THE KEY-LOCK MAN
KID RODELO
KILLOE
KILRONE
KIOWA TRAIL
LANDO
THE LONELY MEN

THE MAN CALLED NOON
THE MAN FROM THE
  BROKEN HILLS
THE MAN FROM SKIBBEREEN
MATAGORDA
MOJAVE CROSSING
MUSTANG MAN
NORTH TO THE RAILS
OVER ON THE DRY SIDE
THE QUICK AND THE DEAD
RADIGAN
REILLY'S LUCK
RIDE THE DARK TRAIL
THE RIDER OF LOST CREEK
RIVERS WEST
SACKETT
THE SACKETT BRAND
SACKETT'S LAND
SHALAKO
SILVER CANYON
SITKA
THE SKY-LINERS
TAGGART
TREASURE MOUNTAIN
TUCKER
UNDER THE SWEETWATER RIM
WAR PARTY
WESTWARD THE TIDE
WHERE THE LONG GRASS BLOWS

Louis L'Amour
Guns of the
Timberlands

BANTAM BOOKS
TORONTO · NEW YORK · LONDON

GUNS OF THE TIMBERLANDS
*A Bantam Book / published by arrangement with
the author*

PRINTING HISTORY
Jason Press edition published June 1955
Bantam edition / November 1955
2nd printing ... November 1955
New Bantam edition / February 1960
18 printings through February 1977

*Bantam Books are published by Bantam Books, Inc. Its trade-
mark, consisting of the words "Bantam Books" and the por-
trayal of a bantam, is registered in the United States Patent
Office and in other countries. Marca Registrada. Bantam
Books, Inc., 666 Fifth Avenue, New York, New York 10019.*

To Edna Lamoore Waldo

GUNS OF THE
TIMBERLANDS

CHAPTER 1

THE TWO RIDERS on the Deep Creek trail had the morning to themselves. Within the range of their attention nothing moved.

The vast sky arched blue and empty to the horizon. Before them the trail was a white, winding line across the face of the desert plain. On both sides of the trail the bunch-grass levels stretched far toward the blue hills, and in the bottoms along Deep Creek were grassy meadows and a scattering of willow and cottonwood.

Behind them, looming suddenly from the desert, was isolated Deep Creek Range, a fifty-square-mile group of mountains. Its lower slopes were naked rock or rock clad with the sparse, dry-land brush of the middle desert. Along the crests there appeared at intervals the darker tufts of pine tops.

Within the rough circle of Deep Creek Range lay the basin of the creek, a high plateau heavily timbered and slashed by the canyons and valleys of Deep and Cave creeks, carrying a fine stand of virgin timber. The high meadows were rich with grass, well watered and green; the inner slopes of the mountains, except for a few places where lightning-started fires had struck, were thickly clad with ponderosa pine and fir.

There was only one road through the Deep Creek Range, a long abandoned trail used by west-bound pioneers and later, briefly, by a stage line. No wagon had used that road in many years, only the riders of the B-Bar.

"New folks in town." Bill Coffin volunteered the information after three miles of silence and chill morning. "A good-lookin' blonde."

Clay Bell drew on his cigarette, found it dead, and after pinching it to be sure, tossed it into the desert. Here there was no danger of fire but the habit remained from forest living.

"A couple of lumberjacks," Coffin added. "And some city man . . . all duded up."

"You talk too much." Clay took out the makings and began to build a smoke. He glanced over at Coffin, fine lines of remembered laughter showing at the corners of his eyes. "What would lumberjacks be doing in Tinkersville?"

"Search me." Bill Coffin was a lean, strongly built young cowhand, a good man with a rope or horse. "What would a beautiful blonde do there?"

"You mean you didn't offer any suggestions?"

"No chance. Just seen her, then she was gone."

"Smart girl."

Tinkersville sprawled in ungainly, clapboarded charm on the flatland near the Creek. One street of false-fronted stores, and a half-dozen streets of dwellings, few of them painted, some of adobe. On the outskirts, near some ancient adobe ruins, three youngsters hunted Indians, and from the shouts of "bang-bang" they were having good hunting.

As the two riders neared the outskirts, a big man on a gray horse rode past them, his face stiff.

Coffin grinned at Bell. "Schwabe ain't forgot that whippin' you gave him. Looks mighty unhappy with you."

The street was lazy and sun-filled. A hen picked at an apple core in front of the general store. A dog lay sprawled in the dust, soaking up sun. Two men in high-heeled boots, hats tipped back, sat on the edge of the boardwalk, another leaned against the post of the ramada smoking a cigarette. He slanted his eyes at them and lifted a negligent hand in greeting.

Clay Bell regarded the street with pleasure. He was an easy-going man with the wide shoulders and lean hips of a desert rider, a man who looked cool, competent, and ready, yet one in whom behind the quiet of his eyes the humor lay close to the surface. He wore his gun with the same casual ease that he wore his hat or his shirt.

He knew the people in this town and he liked them. He had come here a stranger, now he was a part of something. It had been a long time before that since he had belonged anywhere or to anything.

A big man in a plaid wool shirt worn outside his pants came out of the Homestake. He wore "high-water" pants, rolled up halfway to his knees, and laced boots. It was the unfailing brand of the lumberjack.

Curiosity tinged with worry touched Bell . . . the only timber within miles of Tinkersville was on his own place, at Deep Creek.

A clatter of running hoofs sounded on the loose planks of the bridge at the far end of town, then the rattle of a buckboard. It rounded into the street and a couple of fine blacks brought it down toward the riders at a spanking trot.

The buckboard drew up sharply opposite them, its trailing dust cloud sifting over and around it, then settling into the like dust of Tinkersville's main street.

A big man in laced boots tossed the reins to his companion and sprang lightly from the buckboard. His dark, well-tailored suit and white, stiff-brimmed hat were in marked contrast to the nondescript range clothes of the men along the street.

There was hard, brusque confidence in the way he came toward them. His every action spoke of impatience and assurance. He had seen Clay Bell sitting his horse and had noted the B-Bar brand.

He lifted a hand. "You, there!"

Bill Coffin nudged Bell. "Look what's comin'," he said softly. "Wants to make talk."

The big man's smooth-shaven, white-skinned face was eastern, but Bell knew instinctively this man was no tenderfoot. Not, at least, in the usual acceptance of the term. Bell waited, his lean face offering nothing, his eyes measuring the man.

"Are you Bell?"

Several passers-by drifted to a halt and turned hopefully toward the loud voice. There was a challenge and tone in the voice that seemed to promise trouble, and the citizenry of Tinkersville were interested in trouble. Aside from vague talk of gold prospects, cattle prices, and the way somebody carried on at somebody else's dance, there was little to talk about.

Clay Bell let the man come up to his horse before he replied. Even then he held it a little, letting the man look up at him. "That's my name," he said.

He struck a match on the pommel and lifted it to his cigarette, cupping the match in his left hand. He did not move the right hand, which was a way he had. Old Sam Tinker had noticed that way, and knew what it meant. Bill Coffin had drawn his own conclusions.

Bell waited deliberately, not liking the stranger or his abrupt manner. He had crossed the street as if he owned it, addressed Bell as if he were a Digger Indian.

"You're the man who runs those B-Bar cattle up on Deep Creek?"

"I reckon." Clay studied the man calmly, noting the strong, almost brutal jaw, the powerfully boned face, and the taut white skin. There was no warmth in the eyes. They were impatient eyes, domineering.

"Well, get 'em out of there! I'm logging off that mountain and the flatland beyond it. Starting next week."

"My cattle like it there." Bell studied the end of his cigarette. "I'm not figuring on moving them as long as they are happy. As for logging off that piece, you aren't going to, now or any other time."

He spoke quietly, but with a cool confidence that irritated the big man. Clay Bell had his own brand of assurance, and he had won it along trails far from Tinkersville.

He sat his saddle now, linking the warmth of the morning sun after the chill of the early ride. He liked the town, the shabby red of the brick buildings, the two squat, powerful structures of gray stone, and the jerry-built stores, false-fronted and clapboarded that made up the rest of it. He even liked the worn and polished hitch rails, the shadows under the awnings. After a long time of belonging nowhere, he had come to rest here, and he liked it.

"Probably you don't know who I am." The stranger's smile was tolerant. "I'm Jud Devitt."

Clay looked at him through his cigarette smoke, his eyes faintly amused. "Well, now! That's right interesting, I expect. Only I never heard of Jub Debit. And as far as those cows are concerned, I don't imagine it would make much difference if I had."

The spectators chuckled, and one man laughed outright. Devitt's lips tightened with anger and his face flushed. He had become used to being treated with respect, and the cool assurance of the cattleman annoyed him.

"Whether you've heard of me or not," he said harshly, "you get those cattle out of the woods, and get them out now!" He paused. "I won't tell you again."

Clay Bell drew deep on his cigarette and then exhaled, taking his time. Devitt's demand had been wholly unexpected, yet it struck at the core of all his problems. The Deep Creek range was more than just a stretch of land to him, more than grass for his cows. It was life itself. He had never wanted to stop anywhere until he saw Deep Creek, had never felt that he belonged anywhere. He had come to love that land as a man may love a woman. Not any woman, but *the* woman, the one woman.

None of this showed in his face. He had learned to live without showing what he felt. Seconds had passed. He looked past his cigarette at Jud Devitt and he smiled. "Sorry, friend. I like that land. My cattle like it. They stay."

As he spoke he let amusement show in his eyes, for he had read Jud Devitt, and read him right. Here was a strong, dangerous man, but a man who had won too often, who took himself too seriously. He had no sense of humor that applied to himself, and amusement had the power to irritate him.

Devitt's anger had been mounting. The grins of the spectators annoyed him, and the faint twinkle in Bell's eyes stirred his fury. "One of these days," he said, anger overcoming his good sense, "somebody will pull you off your horse and slap some sense into you!"

Clay smiled and put his palms on the saddle horn. "Want to try it now, mister?"

Jud Devitt had turned and started away. Now he halted in mid-stride. He turned slowly and looked back at Bell, his momentary anger gone, his eyes icy.

"When the time comes, cowboy, I'll do it. And when I do it, the job will be well done, I promise you!" Then he strode back to his buckboard.

Clay Bell watched him go. Not many men would walk away from such a direct challenge, and even fewer could do it and leave the impression Jud Devitt was leaving. Not one person who saw him walk away had any idea that he was dodging a fight. He was simply not ready.

The man was big, too. At least thirty pounds heavier than Clay's one-ninety.

Clay studied the situation, reviewing it in his mind as he watched the buckboard drive away. "Bill"—he turned suddenly in his saddle—"you drift back to the ranch and tell Hank Rooney to take that bunch of cows off Stone Cup and push 'em up to Deep Creek."

"Sure, Boss," Coffin was reluctant, "only I surely wanted to see that blonde again. Man, was she somethin'!"

"You get back to the ranch. I'll handle the blondes!"

The move from Stone Cup to Deep Creek was not due for two weeks, but it would have a dual effect. It would indicate definitely where he meant to make his stand; and also, if something went wrong, his cattle would have the benefit of that extra two weeks on good grass, where there was plenty of water.

He walked his horse along the street to Tinker House, studying the situation. There were not many ranches in this part of the country, and his was the best range within miles, yet without Deep Creek he could never make a go of it with what remained.

Until he had come to Tinkersville and located on the Deep Creek range, he had been a drifting man. It had been Sam Tinker himself, sitting in his polished chair, one elbow leaning on the arm, a shock of iron-gray hair rumpled and awry on his head, who told him of Deep Creek.

Clay Bell remembered the day he had come down that main street the first time, his horse weary of long trails, his clothes dusty. He drew up and looked down the street and it was no different from any other western town . . . yet he felt different about it.

He had stabled his horse and cared for it; he had a drink and a meal. He had walked along the street, looking at the town, and his eyes had kept straying toward the hills, not too far off.

"Passin' through?"

It was then he had seen Sam Tinker for the first time. A big, fat old man with shrewd eyes who rarely moved from his chair.

"Maybe. . . . What's in those hills?"

Tinker studied him. "Cattleman?"

"Figure to be. I've taken herds over the trail."

"Ride like a soldier."

"I was—cavalry."

Sam Tinker had watched men come and go for more years than he liked to remember. Tinkersville was his town. He had planted the seed and been midwife at the birth. He wanted it to grow, but to grow right.

"Range up there," he indicated the hills, "finest cow country in the world. Thick green grass all summer, no end of water. A man could hold his stock down on the flat until hot weather, then move 'em to the Deep Creek range to top 'em off."

"Who's up there?"

"Nobody. Country's like God left it. Not even a trapper." Tinker shifted his huge bulk in his chair. "Only timber in miles, and too far away from any big forest to make lumbering pay. So there she stands."

When the morning sun broke over the hills he was already high among them, and he found it as Tinker had said, and more. He started his first cabin that morning, finished it and a corral before he returned to town. He had sent for Hank Rooney, and things had moved along.

Until now there had been no break in the steady forward progress of the B-Bar, and there was market for considerable beef right in the country, which had few ranches. There were mines scattered around, and miners ate beef. He could pay running expenses with local sales, so he built his herds.

Jud Devitt seemed sure of himself and he must already

have laid plans to log off the Deep Creek country. And he must have moved very swiftly and silently for Bell not to have heard of the venture.

Swinging down at the Tinker House, Bell pushed through the bat-wing doors into the saloon. Other swinging doors divided the saloon from the hotel lobby. He walked to the bar, noting two wool-shirted men with the bottoms of their overalls turned up to a few inches below the knee.

The nearest lumberjack turned and glanced toward him. He was a burly man with a wide, not unpleasant face, tough and rough, but good-humored. "You sure come close to gettin' your meat-house torn down, cowboy! That was Bully Jud Devitt you were talkin' to!"

"Was it?"

He was occupied with his thoughts of the Deep River range. Nothing must go wrong at this stage. He needed that graze to fatten his stock for market, and if trouble forced him to pull them off that rich grass to the parched and arid flats where the grass was even now going dry and stale, he would lose pounds off every head of stock, and could easily lose some of the stock itself. Weight meant dollars, and he needed money. And there would be no rain on the lowlands for another three months, at least.

The lumberjack was not letting it pass. "Jud, he chaws up men like you! I seen him whup three, four in one stack! When it comes to lumber, land, or woman, Jud gets what he wants, and you can bet your bottom dollar if he says he'll log off Deep Creek, he'll do her!"

"He can be stopped."

"Not him!" The big jack moved closer. "My name's Wat Williams, cowboy, an' I've worked for Bully Jud before. He says he's goin' in after that fir, an' he'll do it! And," the big lumberjack grinned insolently, "he'll have fifty of the toughest lumberjacks in the country back of him!"

Bell downed his drink and turned from the bar. Wat Williams grinned at him. There was tough good humor in him and a love for fighting. He had wide shoulders and big hands, and he had just put two stiff drinks behind his belt.

"Bell"—he moved out into the room—"I'd like to take up that offer you made the Boss—*right now!*"

He spoke and he swung. Clay had seen the intent before the blow started, He had seen it in the way the man moved out into the room, and the way his feet were set. As Williams swung, Clay stepped inside and smashed a left and right to the face. The left caught Williams on the eye as he stepped in, but the right landed too far back. Wat was shaken, but he tried to grapple. Bell stepped away, and as Williams moved in, he feinted, then smashed a cracking right to the jaw. It nailed Williams on the button as he was stepping in and he dropped on his face in the sawdust as if hit with an axe.

Bell looked across the fallen man at his companion, but the lumberjack at the bar stared without speaking, as if unwilling to believe his eyes. Turning, Bell went through the swinging doors into the hotel lobby.

Ed Miller looked up from his ledger, observing the skinned knuckles and drawing his own conclusions. He was a taciturn man with no past that anyone knew about. He possessed a faculty for knowing almost everything that happened in Tinkersville without showing any evidence of interest.

He had seen the brief meeting of Devitt and Bell in the street. There were lumberjacks in the bar. Something had fallen hard. Clay Bell had a split knuckle and no evidence of other damage. The conclusion was obvious.

"Has Hardy Tibbott come back yet?"

Miller shook his head. "Not yet, Clay. He's overdue. Nobody has come to town but that lumberman, nobody except the Rileys. Judge James J. and his daughter."

Clay Bell hesitated, his hands on the counter. It was time Hardy was back. Could the delay have anything to do with Devitt? The idea disturbed him, and he stood irresolute, wondering about his best move.

"You should see that Riley girl, Clay!" Miller kept his voice low, "Man, if I was a young sprout like you I'd move in."

"A blonde?"

CHAPTER 2

COLLEEN RILEY saw the man standing at the hotel desk turn and glance up the stairs. Something in the strongly cut face held her attention, then their eyes met and she felt something turn over inside of her. A moment, time for a long breath, and then she continued down the steps.

Her chin lifted, her eyes straight before her, she stopped at the desk beside him. She was sharply aware of the man's hands lying on the register. One knuckle, she observed, was skinned. But the hands were strong and well made.

"Did Mr. Devitt go out?"

"Yes, ma'am." Ed Miller's eyes were without guile. "I believe Mr. Bell here saw him, didn't you, Clay?"

Reluctantly, she faced him. "Could you tell me if he has left yet? Or is he around somewhere?"

"A large—rather forceful gentleman?" Clay's expression was almost too innocent. "With a mustache and an opinion?"

Colleen's lips tightened, but she felt a little ripple of amusement. The description was, she admitted, apt. "I believe that's the man. Did you see where he went?"

"He had a sort of argument. Some ill-bred cowhand, no doubt. Then he got into a buckboard and drove away."

She studied him, sensing the humor but not certain what it might mean. "You'd better tell that cowhand," she said coolly, "that he'd best mind his ways. Mr. Devitt can be very fierce when angry."

"Mr. Devitt is new here," Bell assured her. "Maybe he will learn better."

Colleen Riley had lived much among men and felt no hesitancy at talking to strangers. A composed girl, she had known many of her father's friends, and even her years at an eastern school had not made her reticent.

This tall stranger disturbed her. She felt she should go

11

on, but she disliked to leave what she did not quite understand.

She had seen him first from the head of the stairs, noting
the broad shoulders under the sun-faded blue shirt, the lean
hips and the boots. The gun he wore was no more obvious
than the guns of other men, but it seemed to belong where
it was. He would, she decided, look undressed without it.

That he was unimpressed by Jud Devitt was evident, a
fact that surprised her, for Jud had a way of making his
presence felt and men moved around him with respect.
Even her father treated him with some diffidence. The fact
that this man was not impressed seemed a mute reply to
something she had herself felt—yet she had no reason to
put to the feeling.

"Don't underrate him," she warned him. "Mr. Devitt is
a man who gets things done. He built the railroad through
Slide Canyon, if you remember."

"You seem to know him well."

Her eyes met his, cool and almost defiant. "Yes, we're
to be married."

Somehow the words sounded false, unreal. Yet why
should they? She was going to marry him.

"Are you?"

Again that faint amusement in his voice. Her chin
lifted. "Yes. Yes, I am!"

He looked down at her, gravely serious. She was a
tall girl, five-seven in fact, but his height made her seem
short. "I wish you happiness," he said, then lifted his hat
and walked by her to the door.

Colleen Riley turned on Ed Miller. "Who was that?"

"Clay Bell," Miller said, watching her with bright, curious eyes. "He runs cattle on Deep Creek."

She walked out to the boardwalk and looked down the
street. He was nowhere in sight. Neither, she realized, was
Jud Devitt.

The full significance of Miller's remark reached her
then. This was the man who had the cattle Jud was going
to move!

She took a step, then paused. Moving those cattle might
not be as easy as Jud seemed to believe. There was some-

thing about the tall young cattleman that made her feel he was not a man who could be run over with Jud's usual heedless tactics.

Her eyes found Wat Williams then. The big lumberjack was trying without much luck to hide his face behind an awning post, and with reason. One eye was black and swollen and there was a welt on his jaw.

"Wat! You've been fighting again!"

Wat Williams gave up his attempted concealment. "Ma'am, that was the shortest fight on record. I swung at him and missed. He swung at me and didn't!"

"Does Jud know about this?"

"Not yet, but he had him a run-in with the same feller. They had some words about this land Jud's goin' to log, an' Jud, he threatened to pull this feller off his horse and teach him a lesson. The feller told him to have at it."

Wat worked his jaw, touching it tenderly with his fingertips. "Ma'am, this man ain't goin' to be so easy as Jud figures."

She remembered the split knuckle, and the man's casual indifference to Devitt. "This man—was his name Bell? Clay Bell?"

"That's him. Tall feller, steps mighty easy on his feet, and," he added grimly, "hits hard!"

Wind stirred the street's hot dust. A fly buzzed lazily against a windowpane and sleepy horses stood hipshot at the rails.

There was nothing to see in Tinkersville. It was just a sprawling small town with some ancient buildings of gray stone, and a few of red brick; the rest of the stores and houses were gray, wind-worried clapboard buildings, sun-dried and unpainted. Out on the plains dust-devils danced and the heat waves shimmered like clear liquid.

Colleen Riley walked down the boardwalk to the end of the street. In the distance the mountains looked cool and attractive. She stood staring out over the vast expanse of plain and desert, listening to the desultory talk of western men. A horse stamped to free his hocks of flies, and distantly, from across town, a hammer rang on an anvil.

Tinkersville—heat-baked, nondescript, cut off, what was there in such a place to hold the lives of men? Why would anyone choose such a place when there were New York, London, and Paris?

A deeper blue in the far mountain range indicated a canyon . . . where did it lead to? A meadow? A lake? Some forest fastness where no man had been?

She turned away and looked again at the town. The man at the hotel had told her of Indian wars and cattle trouble, of gun battles and struggles to live, yet the town showed no obvious scars.

Some of those early men had gone on, but others had stayed. That big old man who founded the town—Sam Tinker. She must talk to him.

Tall men stayed . . . short men . . . but strong men. Men with skin like saddle leather and clear eyes that saw beyond today.

These men who stayed had not been wealthy men, but they had been steadfast men, confident men, strong with an inner strength that knows not defeat. Such men had built this town, had kept it alive, and would make it grow. Jud was such a man, building and shaping a new world—or was he?

Was it old Sam Tinker who had said, "Two kinds of men here, Judge Riley. Them that come to build, and them that come to get rich and get out."

Walking back toward the hotel, she glanced through a space between the buildings. Far off, against the blue of distance, a feather of dust lifted, marking the trail of a rider.

Clay Bell? Or was it some other horseman returning to the quiet hills?

Men talked and she listened to the even cadences of their voices. A name caught at her attention and her steps slowed. "Clay? Knowed him since he was a boy, 'cept for the time he was in the war. He was man-growed at fourteen, skinnin' mules with a freight outfit on the Santa Fe Trail.

"Out o' Tennessee by way o' Texas. He rode with Nelson Story on the first cattle drive to Montana."

The other man muttered something, and the older man replied. "Mebbe. He rode with the Rangers, down Texas way. With McNelly. Men with the bark on, them Rangers."

She wanted to listen, but walked on. Shadows were gathering along the faraway hills, and she remembered the music in what the old man said: "Out o' Tennessee by way o' Texas. Man-growed at fourteen, skinnin' mules on the Santa Fe Trail."

What memories came to such a man? What women had he known? Dark-eyed girls in Taos and Santa Fe? Indian girls?

She brought up sharply, her hand on the hotel door. He might be married! He might have children . . . he might be . . . But what difference could it make to her? Only, she would hate to see him lose his home if there were children. That, she told herself, was the only reason the thought disturbed her. There could be no other reason.

Out of Tennessee, by way of Texas.

CHAPTER 3

'JUD DEVITT got down from the buckboard at the station. Bob Tripp, his foreman, was standing on the platform checking the unloading of some heavy machinery from flat-cars. Jud watched for several minutes while he chewed his black cigar and thought. Then he motioned Tripp to one side.

"Bob, I've had words with a cattleman named Bell. He runs stock on that range we're going to log. We may have trouble, so have the boys primed for it. If that cowboy thinks he can keep me out of the stand of timer he's mistaken!"

Tripp nodded. He had worked a dozen jobs with Jud Devitt and enjoyed a good fight. He was an older man, and a tough one who knew how to handle men and get results.

"The boys need it. They got bees in their britches." He glanced at Devitt. "How about the land? That's government property, isn't it?"

"Don't worry," Devitt replied confidently. "Frank Chase is in Washington now. He'll handle that end. Our job is cutting timber." He smiled. "We may have the place logged off before he gets it fixed, but who's to stop us? This is an age, Bob, when the strong man gets what he goes after. This country likes enterprise! It was made for it! A man never gets rich standing still. Plan carefully, then go ahead and let nothing stand in your way."

Bob Tripp did not reply. Jud Devitt got things done, and they were things somebody had to do. Bob Tripp was the man who could get them done for him, and he liked the doing. Nevertheless, being a small man himself, he sometimes had his moments of doubt. To make one man big, many good men had to fall. . . . How would he feel about it if he was one of those under the axe?

"Paid off so far, hasn't it?" Devitt asked, as if reading

his thoughts. "No man has the right to stand in the way of progress."

"This here Bell," Tripp said tentatively, "I've heard some about him. Can't you buy him out?"

"Buy him out?" Devitt gave an incredulous laugh. "You must be getting old, Bob. When did we ever buy a man off government range? He'll get off peaceably or we'll run him off!"

He turned on his heel and started back to the hotel, leaving the buckboard for Tripp. That stand of fir was the finest in the state, and if all went well he would have it off the mountain before the government acted. There was no need to worry about that. Chase was his legal and political fixer, Chase understood how he operated, and Chase knew the right people and how to reach them. He would have the deal fixed up, but there was no use wasting time sitting around when there could be but one answer.

Of course, there had been a time, the Charleston Mountain affair, when Chase had failed. By the time Devitt knew of his failure the mountain was logged off and his men had moved on to another job. A little skillful placing of money had covered that up. They were too busy in Washington to investigate the claims every rancher made, but if a man had money and a little influence almost anything could be done.

The country was bursting with natural resources and the thing to do was get rich while they lasted. It was patriotic, in one sense. He was helping to build the country, and if he got rich in the process, wasn't that the American way? Or was it merely his own way?

A vague thought filtered into his mind that perhaps the natural resources of a nation were for the benefit of all, but he put the thought aside and went on down the street, planning as he walked.

This Bell, now. The man would fight, probably, not realizing how hopeless it was. He had twelve hands, and that would not be nearly enough. The Deep Creek range was wide and deep, and there must be a score of ways he could get into it and start cutting without trouble. In any event, he had fifty tough lumberjacks spoiling for trouble, and if need be he could get as many more.

He had taken time to check on Bell. The man had no cash resources. In fact, he owed money. If he made trouble, there would be more than one way to force him off his ranch.

Riley was here, and that was another asset. It always paid to have one's own judge. It was the first thing he had done —to have Judge Riley appointed Federal Judge in the district. If it came to a court fight, that gate was already closed.

He had talked to the R&R, too. The railroad was eager for the lumbering to start, for it would result in good business for them during a slack time. That was another thing he and Chase had handled. They had not talked to local people, but had gone to the head office, right to the top, in New York. The local people would have their orders to cooperate. If Bell gave him trouble he would see that he got no cars to ship his cattle.

Chewing his cigar, he went over the details again. He could find no loophole left open for Bell. The rancher had his tail in a crack. No getting around that.

He chuckled. Imagine the nerve of the fellow! Offering to fight *him!* At the time he had been angry, but now it amused him. Might be fun, at that. But it could wait.

Too tall—couldn't weigh over one-seventy. If Bell wanted it, he could have it.

He walked quickly along the street, scarcely noticing the people along the walk. There was a lot to do, but things were moving.

Wat Williams was still loafing on the street, and Jud saw his black eye. He stopped abruptly, and Williams explained, reluctantly.

Devitt was suddenly irritated. He did not care how much his men fought, but he wanted them to win. "Don't worry! You'll get another chance at him!"

"If you don't mind," Williams said mildly, "I've had mine. You can have him, or anybody else. Me, I'm satisfied!"

Jud Devitt brushed by him and went into the hotel dining room.

Clay Bell's B-Bar ranch lay in the open mouth of a lovely green valley that yawned widely into the flat that sloped up from the bottom where Tinker's Creek ambled placidly over the sand.

The ranch lay around a shoulder of the mountain from the town, and some miles away. It could not be seen from the town, but the green of the grass where the valley opened was plainly visible. The ranch buildings lay a good mile farther up the canyon on a long bench under the brow of the hills.

From the wide and deep veranda of the ranch house the view stretched away for miles, past the bed of Tinker's Creek and past the land that lay below the town. In late fall, winter, and spring, cattle could be grazed on those flatlands, but the number of acres per cow was too few, and without the excellent graze, water, and hay meadows of the upland valleys, no rancher could hope to succeed.

The timber of the Deep Creek country was excellent; it was virgin timber and there was little undergrowth. Not until it had been cut over would brush invade those woodland parks to crowd out the grass.

Clay Bell was grazing six thousand head of cattle, and of that number the greater part fed on the plateau behind the ridge. By carefully culling his herds and beefing the culls, he had built a fine mixed herd of white-face and shorthorn cattle, but his planning had exceeded his income and he had borrowed heavily, mortgaging his herds.

Another year would see him free of his indebtedness and ready to increase his herds and to drill some wells on the flatlands where the prospects of water were good. But as he rode homeward he was considering the situation that now existed due to the arrival of Jud Devitt.

The man had strength and force of character, he had the confidence born of victory, and Clay had seen the eagerness for battle manifest in the readiness with which

Williams had attacked him. Devitt would have more money with which to fight, and more men.

Once he had scouted the Deep Creek range and knew what lay before him, Bell had gone into his ranching with care. Times were changing. New men were coming west and the land would not always be free.

Two other men had preceded him, briefly, on Deep Creek. Chuck Bullwinkle had filed in a claim high up on the slopes of Piety Mountain above the creek. The creek itself flowed from a small cave on Bullwinkle's place, and Clay's first step had been to buy that claim. Chuck Bull-winkle was tired of the loneliness and sold his own claim and another he had bought from a former partner.

Later, Bell bought another claim that straddled an old wagon route through the ridge that spread out in two directions from Black Butte. This range of mountains formed the far wall of the Deep Creek valley, opposite Piety Mountain. The result of these purchases left him in sole possession of the only two passes giving access to the inner plateau. They also left him in possession of the principal source of water.

Yet he was worried now. Logging off of the mountain and plateau would ruin him. Even the process of logging would force him to move his cattle off the Deep Creek range and back to the parched flatlands. Once the trees were gone, the washing away of the topsoil would ruin the plateau and the valley for grazing. Encroaching brush would finish it for good.

If forced to sell now, he could sell nothing but his cattle. When his debts were paid and his hands paid off, he would have nothing left for six years of hard work and planning.

He had not intentions of selling, but it was like him to consider all the facets of his problem. That he was in for a knockdown and drag-out fight, he knew. A shrewd judge of men, he did not take Devitt lightly. Jud was a man accustomed to victory and a man who would stop at nothing to win.

Hank Rooney, Bell's foreman, was waiting for him.

"Got the boys out shoving them cows up from Stone Cup," Hank said. "What's happened?"

Briefly, and without hedging, Bell explained the situation. "It's war, Hank. Unless I miss my guess, it's a war to the death. He struck me as a tough, smart man."

"Well," Rooney spat, "things been sort of quiet, anyway. Will it be a shootin' war?"

"Later, maybe. First it will be a war of strategy. Maybe he's got it on me there. This won't be my kind of fight, to start."

Rooney considered that. He was a man pushing fifty, and no stranger to trouble. "You suppose he knows you've blocked the only two ways into this country?"

"Doubt it. We'll play a waiting game. He's got men that he's got to feed and house. First, we'll get some fat on our cows. We might have to sell some for fighting money."

Hank looked dourly down the valley. "Bill Coffin said he seen Stag Harvey and Jack Kilburn in town. You want to hire them boys?"

"Too much blood behind 'em, Hank. I don't want shooting if it can be avoided."

Hank prodded at a rock with his toe. He was a lean, tall man, looking older than his years. He had come west with a herd from Ogallala, and before that had punched cows in Wyoming, Arizona, Nevada, and Utah. He was a veteran of three sheep and cattle wars, and although by no means a gunman, he was a tough old puncher who knew how to fight.

"I say if they want fight, give it to 'em." He looked up. "What's next, then?"

"Fall some logs and build a barricade across The Notch. That's their best route to the plateau."

Hank Rooney spat. "Reckon he knows about The Notch? Makes a man figure some. How come he knowed about this place, anyway? Nobody's been around, no strangers, anyway."

"Somebody told him about this timber," Bell said. "It had to be a local man. But even the local men don't know I filed on this land. At least, I don't think they know. I rode all the way to the capital to file, and I doubt if there are four cattlemen in the state who have actually filed on or bought land. They merely squatted and started to run cows, claiming the land by living on it."

Bell stripped the saddle from his mount. "I'd like to know who tipped him off. Have we got enemies, Hank?"

"Schwabe don't cotton to us much. And it's a cinch Devitt didn't fall into this by accident. It looks like he came all primed to strip the logs off this range. Wonder if he's made a deal with the government?"

Clay Bell walked to the veranda and sat down. He built a smoke while mentally reviewing the approaches to Deep Creek. The only two routes belonged to him. For a time he could deny access to the inner valley. But if Devitt acquired a right from the government he could not legally refuse right of way across his ranch.

He must think of everything first, to be ready, then sit tight and let Devitt make the first move. When he started there would be time enough to stop him. If he wanted to play rough—well, there was no man among the dozen employed by B-Bar who had not played rough before. His crew was small, but they were fighting men.

His ranch buildings lay athwart the entrance to Deep Creek by way of Emigrant Gap. The long abandoned road had passed through the Gap and across to leave by The Notch. Devitt might know of the road, for the existence of the timber had been made known to him somehow. This was not timber country; therefore Devitt had to have a local informant.

Sitting on the veranda, Bell examined the situation. The house was built of native rock and had walls three feet thick. There were five rooms—living room, kitchen, two bedrooms, and an office. The house was surrounded on all sides by the veranda, low-roofed and cool, and shaded by several huge old trees. When Bell ate at home, which was not often, he preferred to sit on the veranda where he could look down the valley. Nobody could approach from the valley side without being long under observation from the house.

The house stood at one corner of a rectangle of ranch

buildings and corrals. East and north of the house lifted
sheer walls of rock. No more than thirty yards from the
house was the stone chuckhouse known as the "wagon."
Beyond it, separated by about thirty feet, was the long,
low, stone bunkhouse, and at the far end of the rectangle
was another stone building divided into separate rooms.
These were respectively the saddle and harness room, the
tool house, the storeroom, and the blacksmith shop. The
other side of the rectangle was a long stone barn with a
loft filled with hay, and three corrals, two on one side of
the barn, one on the other.

The stone buildings of the ranch effectually blocked
all access to Deep Creek through Emigrant Gap unless
two gates were opened by ranch personnel. One of these
gates was between two of the stone ranch buildings.

Deep Creek plateau and the valley lay seven hundred
feet higher than the ranch itself. That seven-hundred-foot
rise was covered in two miles of trail, the last half-mile
through a canyon that was a veritable bottleneck.

Bell paced the veranda restlessly. Despite the suggestion
that Morton Schwabe might have been Devitt's informant,
he did not believe it. Schwabe was essentially a small-
calibered man. Owning a small ranch, Schwabe would
willingly do almost anything to injure Bell, but he would
scarcely think of a thing like this.

Uneasily, he accepted the realization that behind this
move lay another force, someone who had brought Jud
Devitt into the country for his own reasons. Someone who
had his own plans against Bell.

Hank Rooney was already at the table in the chuckwagon when Clay walked in. "Boss," he said, "we might
send Rush and Montana over to The Notch right away."

"Good idea. Rifles and plenty of grub, but no shooting if it can be avoided—but no trespassing, either."

"And if they show up?" Rush Jackson was a bow-
legged puncher from the Big Bend country of Texas.

"Send up a smoke. A straight smoke that they're coming, and a single puff for every five men or less. We'll have
a man on Piety Mountain to relay the signal."

During the excited talk that followed, Clay Bell ate in

silence. There had been no trouble for him in Tinkersville, and he had hoped there would be none. He turned
the matter over in his mind, trying to decide what the
best solution would be. But his mind refused to cope with
the problem. Instead, he kept thinking of Colleen Riley.

When supper was finished he walked out on the porch
and looked down the long valley. A faint rose still showed
along the serrated ridges of the mountains beyond, but soft
shadows gathered in the valley, and in the stillness of
early evening sounds were magnified.

Somewhere out there a quail called, and there was a
rush of wings in the darkness; a lone star had appeared,
bright as a close-up lantern or a signal fire. The star hung
in the Prussian blue of the sky above the mountain ridge,
the last remaining light.

This was no country for fighting. It was a country for
peace, for homes—but he rightly guessed there would be
little peace for him in the time just ahead, and few eve-
nings again when he could look with content upon the
empty stillness of the valley.

Was she really in love with Jud Devitt? Certainly, he
must seem an attractive man, and he was one with a repu-
tation for success. He was no simple cattleman, but a
man from her own world, a man who got things done.

Clay rubbed his cigarette out on the stone sill and was
turning away when Bill Coffin stopped and called out,
"Boss, did you see that blonde?"

"No—the one I saw was a redhead."

CHAPTER 4

IN THE BANK at Tinkersville, Noble Wheeler hitched his heavy, corpulent body around in the swivel chair to face his visitor. That Jud Devitt was upset was obvious.

Devitt dropped into the chair across the desk from Wheeler and put his white hat on the desk. His black hair was parted to perfection and plastered down to his skull. He had a square face and a head like a block of granite. This morning his eyes were hard and impatient. Jud Devitt liked a good fight but there were aspects to this one that did not appeal to him.

Victory had become the usual thing for Devitt, and he had grown to be impatient of those who challenged his decisions or delayed his success. The present move depended much on speed of accomplishment, and he was in no mood to be thwarted. Especially, with Colleen Riley in the gallery.

Clay Bell had not been frightened. He had not only had the nerve to challenge Devitt openly, but had publicly whipped one of his toughest lumberjacks. That Colleen was obviously interested in the man was an added irritation.

"About this man Bell," Devitt began abruptly. "You hold his paper, and he's going to be an obstacle to our realizing on that timber. He refused to move his cattle, and if you can't influence him to move them, we'll have to do it for him."

Wheeler shifted his heavy body and spat into the cuspidor. Thoughtfully, he chewed at the corners of his yellowed mustache. "No," he said finally, "I can't butt in. I tipped you off to this timber, but there's no way I can come into the open.

"Pullin' his cows off that range will break Bell, an' everybody knows it. You're here only until you log off the timber; I'm here for good. Anything I do will have to be done under cover."

"Suppose he wants a renewal on his loan?"

"That I can refuse. I can tell him that with you in the picture he has become a bad risk."

Devitt nodded. "That will do nicely. He's going to need money for this fight."

He started to rise, but Wheeler lifted a staying hand. "You know anything about this here Bell?"

"What should I know?" Devitt was impatient. "He's in my way, that's all I need to know."

"You sit down, Jud. Sit down an' listen to me. I got a stake in this, too." Wheeler put his fat hands on his chair arms and leaned forward. "You're a smart man, Devitt. You get things done, and I like that. You ain't particular about ways and means, and I like that, too. But don't make any mistakes about this man Bell. He's a fighter."

"Fighter, is he?" Devitt laughed without warmth. "I'll give him plenty of fight!"

"You listen to me! Bell was fightin' Comanches when he was fourteen. Then he was in New Orleans a while, doin' I don't know what. After that he was a Texas Ranger two years, and then in the cavalry durin' the War Between the States.

"Got to be a major. After the war he rode with trail herds, hunted buffalo, and prospected the goldfields up to Bannock an' Alder Gulch. This man knows how to fight and when to fight."

Jud Devitt was all attention now, watching Wheeler closely and taking in every word. He was conscious of irritation again. Why hadn't he been told all this before? The man might be dangerous . . . the fact that he had been a major showed something—either ability to command, or friends in the right places. In either case, Bell could be dangerous.

"Those who know this man Bell says he's a gunfighter. He's never throwed a gun on anybody hereabouts, but that's no proof. An' don't think he's alone! That Hank Rooney is an old curly wolf off the dry range. Rush Jackson was a Ranger in the same outfit with Bell, and Montana Brown was a sergeant in Bell's command durin' the war."

"We'll have the law," Devitt assured him, "and I've the men and the money. This contract for ties to the Mexican Central is juicy enough, and the saving in transportation will more than pay the cost of rooting Bell out of there."

Jud Devitt walked out into the sunlight. He bit off the end of a cigar and lighted it, squinting against the sun. He felt good; the prospect of a fight always gave him a lift. Bell would be more dangerous than he had believed, and he would have friends, too.

That was the worst of it with western men. A man never knew what he might be facing. Nor what a man's background might be. The unshaved man seated next to you on a restaurant bench might have pulled stroke with the Oxford crew. Many adventurous young foreigners had come to the West looking for adventure and excitement, and many of them were fighters who asked no favors from any man.

Devitt's eyes shifted toward the trail that led to the mountains. It would stand up under the weight, all right. Tomorrow he would get his donkey engine and sawmill loaded on the wagons and then he would move right in. The route lay up the old trail through Emigrant Gap, and their move would call Bell's bluff.

He chewed his cigar thoughtfully, watching the street. If this job went as he hoped, this would be the last of his ventures in this country. He was growing now, he was moving out. There was no need for him to restrict himself. In a country like this, a man who used his head could find many opportunities, but he wanted to go east, move in the circles of big financiers. He had ability, and once there he could become as big as any of them.

Bell? He was another cattleman. Tough, perhaps. Jud Devitt chuckled. Tough? He would show him a few tricks. He would teach him how to be tough. And there was no reason for guns—the man had already talked fight with his fists, and when the time came . . .

He scowled, remembering Noble Wheeler. The banker had evidently gone to some length to find out what he knew about Bell. His fund of information was wide and complete. Why? It was a point to be considered.

Jud Devitt knew himself and had no secrets from himself. He was a man unhindered by scruples, a fighter to whom winning was all that could be considered. Ends and means counted for nothing as long as there was no delay and the cost was kept down.

He had planned his moves with care, studying the maps provided by Wheeler, and other maps, less detailed, of the area. He had underestimated Bell, but it would not pay to take too lightly the old man back there in the bank. Noble Wheeler must have something more in his mind than the profits from the tie contract which he would share. Devitt had allowed him only a small percentage of that profit, and Wheeler had accepted too meekly.

How Wheeler had learned of the Mexican Central tie contract, Devitt did not know. Wheeler had come to Santa Fe and made contact with Devitt, explaining that there was plenty of timber, several hundred miles closer than Devitt had believed.

The banker showed his skillfully drawn maps, indicated sources of water, and the old route through Emigrant Gap. Devitt sent Tripp and Williams to cruise the timber without making their presence known. Slipping through The Notch when snow was still on the ground and no cattle had been driven to the high country, they made their survey and got out unseen. Their report was more than satisfactory. The proximity of the timber to the border would almost double the profit to be made on the deal.

Devitt moved swiftly. Immediately he got in touch with Frank Chase, in Washington. Chase set about getting a timber grant for Devitt, but Jud had no plans to await due process of law or the long process of cutting Washington red tape. He had proceeded to move into the area with his equipment, and now he was going to log off Deep Creek; and if his grant did not go through—well, who was to do what?

Rolling his cigar in his lips, he considered the situa-

tion anew. What had he forgotten? Chase would handle
the Washington end. The R&R would refuse cars for
Bell's cattle shipment, and Wheeler would hold back on
future loans. It took money to fight a war, and through
Wheeler he knew Bell's financial position down to the
last dollar.

Clay Bell, riding his palouse toward Piety Mountain,
had come to the same conclusion at which Devitt had arrived. He was going to need money.

He studied the forest with a more attentive eye. It
was a stand of mingled fir and ponderosa pine, and Bell
could appreciate Devitt's problem. Yet these mountains,
once stripped, would be ruined forever as range. The thin
topsoil would wash away, the hills would become bare,
and this island of forest would be gone.

Turning the palouse, he drifted down through the trees
and into a succession of grassy meadows. Already the cattle from the flats had begun to scatter out, walking and
feeding in the rich grass of the well-watered uplands.

Wind stirred the tall grass, and in the distance, above
the rough shoulder of Piety Mountain, an eagle soared. It
was very still. His horse dipped his head and caught up
a mouthful of grass. On the far slope the trim columns of
the fir made a row of bars against any higher advance, a
wall of splendid trees, uniform in size as if cast from a
mold.

It troubled him that he knew so little of that part of
the Deep Creek range which lay beyond the creek and
west of The Notch. In the business of running cattle and
building a ranch there had been little time for explora-
tion. So far as he knew, it was rough and heavily forested
country into which there was neither opening nor outlet
except from across the creek on his own range.

Bell drew up on a little knoll, almost bare of trees. From
his vantage point he could look over the tree tops and see
much of what lay within the circle of mountains.

On his left and just ahead loomed the great mass of
Piety Mountain, and highest point in many miles. Far
away to the west lay the serrated ridge that formed the

far wall of the basin, whose only opening was The Notch. For a long time he studied that range, and studied the tree tops of the area across the creek as if to read what lay beneath them.

A little snow lingered in the cracks and hollows of the mountain, and the wind that came down from the ranges was cool. It was a good country, a man's country. At the thought of it lying waste and barren, stripped of those magnificent trees, he felt a sharp pang. This was virgin timber, untouched by man, but scarred in places by fires created by lightning.

Since he had taken over the range he had established a fire watch on Piety, and a dozen times in the past few years all hands had come out to fight fire. Usually they had managed to put out blazes with a quick rush of riders and some hot, fast work. But once they had fought fire for days, and he had hired extra men from the town to help put out the blaze.

He rode on now, taking the long trail that led up the mountain, sometimes under the trees, occasionally out on the open side of the mountain. Once he saw a mountain lion, and a dozen times he came upon deer trails.

Bill Coffin was on duty atop Piety when he rode up to the shelter on the peak. "Rider comin'," Coffin said. "Looks like a woman."

He was a lean, well set-up young man with blond hair and a thoughtful face. A quiet man, but tough and capable.

Coffin offered his glasses and Clay studied the rider with interest. The morning air was clear and the sun bright, but along the trail from town there were occasional clumps of smoke trees and desert willow that obscured the rider for minutes at a time. Finally, as she emerged from behind a sandhill, he made her out. It was Colleen Riley.

There was a steep trail, useful only to a skilled rider on a good mountain horse, that led off Piety on the town side. He handed the glasses back to Coffin. "I'm going down there."

He started his horse, then turned in the saddle. "Devitt will probably start moving today."

The sun was warm and he tipped his hat lower over his face. He went swiftly down the dangerous switchback trail, sliding the last few feet, then breaking into a canter through the cat-claw and mesquite. He came out on the trail just as Colleen appeared, not twenty yards away.

"Hello, cowboy!" she called gaily. "Riding somewhere?"

"To meet you." He gestured toward Piety. "Saw you coming."

She glanced toward the peak, then looked back at him, her eyes sober. He looked fit and handsome this morning, a lean, powerful man who filled out his gray wool shirt as a man should.

"We've been expecting visitors," he added, "and did not want to seem lacking in hospitality."

"Clay"—she used his first name without thinking—"you mustn't have trouble with Jud. He's a hard man—too hard sometimes. Why don't you sell out to him?"

"He hasn't asked me. If he did, I wouldn't sell. This is my home, and I like it here. I'm not going to tuck in my tail and run at the first sign of trouble. And I've had trouble before."

Her eyes followed the trail toward the buildings in the mouth of the Gap. "You've a lovely view."

He swung his horse into the trail and they rode along. "It was the view I liked as much as the grass," he admitted. "I like space out in front of me."

Colleen drew up suddenly. "Why! Why, the trail goes right through your gates!"

Clay Bell dug out the makings and began to build a smoke, offering no comment.

She turned on him. "Jud will have a lot of trouble getting his machinery through those gates, won't he?"

Bell looked up at her, grinning slyly. "Yes, ma'am, I sort of think so."

"You won't let him?"

"That's right."

"But you don't own the timberland!"

"Neither does Jud. But I've a prior right of use. I've

even worked to improve it, and to prevent fires. He wants to destroy all we've saved."

She turned in the saddle. "But you don't understand! The ties are for a railroad, and railroads build a country."

"So does beef."

For the first time she began to see the situation in its true light. She had known Jud Devitt three years and had become accustomed to seeing him ride roughshod over obstacles. Looking suddenly at Clay Bell, she had a sudden realization he presented a different sort of obstacle. One that might not be so easy to ride over.

"There'll be trouble," she said soberly. "Serious trouble."

"Colleen"—he gestured at the ranch, then down at the bottom lands—"this wasn't easy to build. Without the water and grass from the high range, we can't operate here. I'd be broke. I'd be through.

"I fought Indians and rustlers when I first came in here. Two of my first bunch of hands are buried here. You think I'm going to give up just because Jud Devitt wants to log off my land?"

They rode on and Hank Rooney opened the gate for them, glancing briefly at Colleen.

"Won't you come in?" Clay said. He turned without waiting for her reply. "Hank, tell that cook to rustle us some coffee. We'll be on the porch."

When they were seated she looked around with excited interest. The ride and the early air had brought color to her cheeks. He watched her with appreciation. There was depth to her, and a quickness of mind that he liked. Young as she was, she was no child. She was a woman with all a woman's instincts. He felt a vague uneasiness stir within him. She was the first woman who had ever sat on this porch, looked out over this view.

"It's strange to actually be out West," she said suddenly. "My uncle used to tell us stories about Bill Longley and John Wesley Hardin. Were there actually men like that?"

"Some still around."

"Do you know Stag Harvey and Jack Kilburn? Are they really dangerous men?"

He looked around at her. "Where did you see them?"

"Oh, they were talking to Bob last night. Mr. Tripp, you know. He's foreman of the lumberjacks for Jud. That clerk at the hotel told me who they were."

The cook came in with the coffee, prepared to be surly about it. Then he saw Colleen and swallowed a little. Carefully, he dried an already dry table before her, and then put down the coffee with a little flourish.

Tripp talking to Harvey and Kilburn? Hiring them? No, he told himself, it was too soon for that. Devitt did not yet know what sort of a fight he was facing. Yet the fact was one to be remembered. Both men were strictly cash-on-the-line warriors. Tough and dangerous, but fighters for money—and worth all they were paid.

He glanced up from his coffee at the girl across the table. It was not only the first time any woman had ever sat on this veranda, but the first time in many months that one had sat across the table from him. Somehow she fitted into the background, she belonged here. She was looking across the valley now, her features relaxed, an expression of quiet peace in her eyes and around her mouth.

She looked around, suddenly aware of his attention. For the first time they looked directly at each other, and everything inside him seemed to come suddenly to rest. A slight flush mounted in her cheeks.

"You belong here." He said it suddenly. "This should be your home."

She studied him curiously, then looked around the ranch yard, at the sunlit, hard-packed earth, the soft shadows along the walls, the coolness of the place after the heat of the valley. Yet even the valley, with its pastel greens and browns, contributed to the peace of the place. She liked the distance, liked the emptiness. She had never been a girl who depended upon others for pleasure, excitement, or entertainment.

His words echoed in her mind, and she felt a little shiver of something almost like fear, yet there was such a ring of sincerity and truth in his voice that it caught every bit of her attention and almost forced her acceptance.

Was this her country? Did she belong here, under the shoulder of Emigrant Gap? There was a faint perfume from the sage that mixed with the aroma of the coffee, the smell of old leather, the clean, bright warmth of the sun.

No sooner had the thought come to mind than she rebelled. What could she be thinking of? She was to marry Jud Devitt!

"You're mistaken," she told him seriously. "I'm a city girl. This is just an interlude for me, a sort of vacation."

His eyes were slightly mocking. "Is it?"

"Jud Devitt is a man a girl could be proud of," she said. "He does things, big things. Men respect him for his ability."

"These big things—aren't they all done for Jud Devitt? And you want to remember that you've only see him win. You never know a man until you see him lose."

She looked at him again and something in his eyes made her heart falter. "And you? Have you ever lost?"

"More than once."

He glanced out from under the edge of the veranda roof. A thin trail of smoke lay against the sky. As he looked there was a puff.

"Jud Devitt's coming now." Bell got to his feet. "I wish he would bring all his men at once. The sooner they know what they are facing, the better."

He held the door for her and they walked outside. The cook rattled pans in the kitchen but there was no one else about.

"Are you so anxious for trouble?"

"No ... but if it has to come, why wait?"

"His men like to fight. They are used to winning, too."

He could see them coming, four men riding toward the Gap. He glanced toward Piety Mountain and saw two more puffs of smoke.

Coolly, he considered his position. It was unlikely that Devitt would try to force a way through at this time. He would try to bully his way through, then resort to trickery or some legal or semi-legal means. But a man with a rifle could hold his place for a long time.

He walked to his saddle and took the rifle from the scabbard.

"You're not going to use that?"

"Not unless I'm forced to." There was a whimsical light in his eye. "Not unless your man tries to come through."

He stood waiting, watching the riders. Jud Devitt was in the lead, and the man rode well. A little behind on his right was Bob Tripp, and the two other men followed close behind. Clay waited. Sweat trickled down his cheek and he drew deep on his cigarette, then dropped it to the earth.

They were coming on, and he was ready. He stepped outside the gate and stood waiting, a tall, lonely figure, the stone walls of the buildings rising to right and left.

CHAPTER 5

DEVITT had not failed, as he approached, to note the way in which the ranch buildings commanded the passage through the Gap. This was something he should have been told. Why had Wheeler failed to tell him?

The slits in the rock walls were ports for shooting, and he could see at a glance that if it came to that sort of fighting, two men could hold the Gap against fifty. His jaw muscles tensed as he saw the figure of Clay Bell standing carelessly outside the gate, waiting.

Then he saw Colleen Riley, and he swore under his breath. What possessed the girl to come out here at a time like this?

Devitt drew up some twenty yards from Bell. "We're scouting a route into the Deep Creek timber," he said. "Can we get our sawmill through here?"

"This way is closed."

"So?" Devitt placed his hands on the pommel. "You undertake to block a public road? A stage route?"

Clay Bell took his time, rolling a fresh smoke before he spoke. He wanted to take time enough for more of his riders to appear. Also, he could see that Devitt was impatient.

"The stage stopped using this route fifteen years ago, and the road goes through Tinkersville now. Nobody has been allowed through here since I took over, without express permission."

Devitt was coldly angry. It irritated him that Colleen must be standing there to see him frustrated. "You take a lot on yourself, Bell. You're just a squatter here. You ranchers try to control the entire range without the slightest legal right."

Clay smiled and put the cigarette between his lips. Deliberately, he stalled. "You're a smart man, Devitt. You should have looked into my land titles before you started this move. I've filed on this claim and proved up on it. I own all the land in Emigrant Gap, lock, stock, and barrel.

"Also," he added, "I own over a hundred acres at the foot of the Pass. You'll not cross over my land with any logging equipment whatever, now or later."

Jud Devitt sat very still in his saddle. For the moment he was beaten, and he tried to think of some way to save face until he could circumvent this move. Noble Wheeler should have told him of this. At the same time, he appreciated a good blow. Clay Bell was shrewd, and Devitt could see no mere show of force would bluff the man.

"You deny me right-of-way? You can't do it, Bell. A man has a right of access to his property. Legally, you haven't a leg to stand on."

Clay drew deep on his cigarette. The wagons hauling Devitt's machinery were drawing nearer. "Possession has its legal points, Devitt. And I'm in possession. Also, I'm grazing cattle on Deep Creek range. Sorry, Devitt, you've tried to stack the cards on the wrong man."

Jud Devitt's patience was wearing thin. "What," he asked harshly, "if we force a way?"

Bob Tripp glanced quickly at Devitt, his lips forming a protest. Devitt was bull-headed sometimes and might not realize what he was facing.

"You won't," Bell replied shortly. "You try to force a way in and you'll have to come shooting."

"There's four of us—one of you."

"Yes."

Jud Devitt studied the man before him. His impatience drove him, and he was angered to have a man standing between himself and the job he meant to do. His every urge was to drive through, to ride the man down and press on. He had three tough men with him, and all were armed. Behind, others came. Yet something held him back.

It was the man himself.

It was Clay Bell, and something in his manner. Bell was neither alarmed nor excited. He gave no indication of any emotion. He just waited for Devitt to move.

Jud Devitt had the feeling suddenly that to Clay Bell this was old, not new. That he played a game in which all the moves were clear-cut and definite, while Devitt himself was uncertain.

"All right," he said finally, "you've stopped me. But I'll log off Deep Creek if it has to be over your dead body!"

He turned his horse but Bell's voice arrested his movement. "Devitt?"

"What?"

"What about your dead body?"

Devitt stared at Bell and suddenly within him there was that cold realization, something that had never really occurred to him before—he might be killed himself! It was preposterous, and yet . . .

"Colleen? Are you riding with us?"

She swung into her saddle and rode to the gate which Bell held open. "Be careful," she whispered. "I know him. He'll stop at nothing!"

At the foot of the grade Jud Devitt stopped beside the wagons. "Hold the wagons," he told Williams. "We'll go up to the plateau later."

"Better send us a chuckwagon. We've only a little grub."

"You won't camp here!" Clay Bell sat the saddle of the appalousa. "This is still my land, Devitt. I'll allow no camping. I'll give you no legal ground at all. Now get rolling! Get back of that white boulder. That's my property line."

Devitt's face was white. "I'll be damned if I—!"

"Move back." There was no comfort in Bell's expression. "Start now or I'll shoot every head of stock on my land. Get started!"

Devitt waved a hand at his men. His face was stiff with fury. "Roll 'em back! Let him have his fun!" He turned on Bell. "You're piling up trouble for yourself!" he said. "I'll see—"

"Move!" Bell repeated. He pushed his horse forward, shouldering his appalousa against Devitt's horse.

Devitt hesitated, his face ugly and mottled; then, never taking his eyes from those of Bell, he backed up until across the line marked by the white boulder.

Promptly, and without a backward glance, Clay Bell swung his horse and cantered up the trail to the ranch house. Jud Devitt stared after him, swore bitterly, then turned his horse toward town. He did not speak to Colleen as they rode along.

He had come off the loser in his first meeting with Bell, but there would be another time . . . another time . . .

"Jud?"

"Oh . . . sorry, Colleen, I'm afraid I wasn't thinking. This mess irritates me."

"Why don't you leave it, Jud? Get the timber another place."

He smiled at her to cover his irritation. "You leave that to me, Colleen. It's my problem."

She rode beside him in silence. She could see he was determined. He was too stubborn to leave now.

"Jud—he'll fight."

"Of course."

"Men will be killed. Doesn't that matter to you?"

"It matters, of course it matters. But one man can't stand in the way of progress. That railroad must go through!"

"You could get the ties elsewhere."

"At greater expense. At greater loss of time. They are here, I mean to have them."

He was scarcely aware of her protests. Already his mind was leaping ahead, trying to find some way to get around this trouble. There might be another route to the Deep Creek range, to both the valley and the plateau. He must talk to Wheeler.

Colleen maintained her silence. The air was cooler now, as they neared town. Dipping down to where the trail ran along the creek, she felt the breeze off the stream, and from the desert willows. She slowed her pace, remembering Clay.

His features were clear-cut, brown from sun and wind. There was something, too, in the way he walked . . . and she had noticed what had impressed Jud Devitt. Clay Bell had not been worried at the thought of trouble. He had wasted no words, indulged in no violent talk. Yet he had won—he had forced Jud Devitt to back up.

And Jud Devitt would never forgive him.

CHAPTER 6

JUD DEVITT found Noble Wheeler in the dining room of the Tinker House. He drew back a chair and dropped into it, coldly furious. "Noble, why didn't you tell me that Clay Bell owned Emigrant Gap?"

Noble Wheeler gripped his fork tightly in one hand, his knife in the other, both big fists resting on the table-top, his big jaws chomping his food like a restless horse over a cold bit. There was no denying the astonishment in his eyes. "What? Did you say owned?"

He put a chunk of beef in his mouth, staring blankly at his plate. Bell owned Emigrant Gap! But that . . .

"He claims he has title to it. Refuses me right-of-way."

"Never guessed he'd be that smart." Wheeler was thinking now. This could change everything, ruin his carefully laid plans. "Changes a lot of things."

"Is there another way up?"

"Through The Notch. T'other side of the plateau."

"Does he own that?" Devitt was sarcastic.

"Maybe. We'll find out."

Devitt pushed back his chair and waved the waitress away. "I'm wiring Chase. If we get our grant on that timber we can force him to give us right-of-way."

"And if you don't?"

Devitt's lips thinned and his eyes looked their dislike at Wheeler. "I'll go in, anyway. No damned cowhand will stop me!"

He did not, Devitt decided, like Wheeler. But he did not have to like him. The banker was tough and shrewd; he had something cooking in his mind that Devitt had not been told. He watched the fat man chomp his food. He was a noisy eater, a glutton. Devitt got up, distaste suddenly sharp within him. Without a word he walked away from the table and went outside.

Suppose he did not get the grant? Then he would have

no legal ground under him at all. Yet Bell's cattle would have to be worked, and he could not keep all his men on guard all the time. There might be still a third way into the Deep Creek area. His thoughts reverted to the grant. He could not back out now, he would not. Grant or no grant, he would have that timber. With Bell busy, there would be a way to get at him. Once they had the timber it wouldn't matter.

He lit a cigar and considered the situation. Cripple Bell. Stop him cold. That was the first thing. It was to be an all-out fight then.

Wheeler's astonishment at the discovery of Bell's ownership had been genuine. Yet there had been something more. Devitt rolled his cigar in his jaws. What did the banker have up his sleeve? Something . . . but what? Jud Devitt had a feeling he was being used as a cat's-paw, and it was a feeling he did not like.

Bob Tripp came up the street, pausing briefly in the door of a saloon across the street. Jud stepped to the edge of the walk.

"Bob! Oh, Bob!"

Tripp turned, trying to locate the voice. Devitt called again.

"Come over! Got something for you!"

Tripp crossed the street and stepped up on the walk. "Looks like a fight, Mr. Devitt," he said. "The boys ain't happy out there, either."

"How many of them are in town? There must be thirty or more."

"About that. What's on your mind?"

"Some of those B-Bar riders will be in town. If a few fights start and some of those boys get hurt, I wouldn't mind at all."

Tripp touched a match to his pipe. "In other words, you want the boys to bust them up? All right, our boys are set for trouble, anyway. What if some of our men are hurt?"

"Pay all the time while recovering. A bonus if Bell gets laid up himself."

Tripp listened, drawing on his pipe. Sometimes he did

not like Jud Devitt, but he could find no better job, and
no better pay. Besides, there was always action, and he
liked action. And one thing you could say for Jud—he
never shied at a fight himself.

"Seen Stag Harvey or Jack Kilburn?"

"Who are they?"

"Gunmen—paid warriors. They're not doing anything
right now."

Jud Devitt looked at the end of his cigar. Killers, then.
Yes, that might come. It was to be avoided if possible, but
the treatment from Bell rankled, and that the man would
shoot he did not doubt. All right then, if they wanted it
that way . . . He was going to have that timber.

"Tell them to stick around town, but don't make any
promises." He took a couple of gold pieces from his vest
pocket. "Give this to them. With my compliments, but
don't make any promises."

A couple of weary riders came up the street. The two
men slumped in their saddles, dusty and tired. Both rode
gray horses, both had B-Bar brands.

"There's a pair of Bell's boys now. I want him short-
handed, Bob."

Tripp took the pipe from his mouth and knocked it out
on the awning post. "All right," he said, and stepped off
the porch and started across the street.

This was a job for Frenchy Duval and Pious Pete Simmons. They would like this. Both men were big, tough,
and known as rough and dirty fighters. Devitt kept them
on the pay roll for jobs like this.

Tripp walked along the street, studying the other horses
at the hitch rails. None were B-Bar brands. Two men . . .
and Bell was reported to have but twelve.

Shorty Jones and Bert Garry had been away from the
ranch for fifteen days. Shorty, blond and pink-cheeked,
almost as wide as he was tall, blinked against the light
in the saloon. Men who rode with him said that Shorty
was as tough as a winter on the Black Rock Desert. Bert
Garry was nineteen, a lanky youngster, but game.

Shorty took the bottle and poured a drink. He tossed

it off, then stood, still holding the bottle while the fiery liquor burned through him. He glanced around at the few men in the saloon.

All were unfamiliar faces. It was early for the usual night crowd, and none of the B-Bar boys were around.

"Jacks," Garry said, low-voiced, "timber beasts. I wonder what's up?"

Shorty filled his glass. "Only timber around here is on Deep Creek, and . . ." His voice trailed off. He thought fast, then dropped a hand on Bert's wrist. "Lay off the whiskey. We're in trouble!"

"What?" Garry looked around, his eyes still red-rimmed from heat and dust. His eyes followed Shorty's warning glance.

Two men had stepped to the bar on each side of the two cowhands. Two more had moved up closer along the bar. All were big, all looked tough.

"Watch it!" Shorty repeated.

Bert Garry was young but he had been over the trail. What was coming he could guess, but he did not know why.

Jones did not lift his eyes from his glass. He spoke just loud enough for Garry to hear. "The only timber is on Deep Creek. The boss wouldn't let no man cut logs up there. We'd better get out of here."

"We'll finish our drinks," Bert said stubbornly.

The lumberjack next to Bert bumped hard against him. Before Garry could turn to speak, Jones caught his arm. He whispered quickly, and Bert Garry caught the idea. Together, muscles poised, they waited. The lumberjacks on either side gathered themselves for a hard lunge at the two cowboys and the one called Frenchy dropped his right shoulder preparatory to driving into Jones. Instantly, Shorty caught Bert's arm and they both stepped back.

It was too late for Duval to catch himself and the sudden disappearance of the cowhand shot his weight into the empty space, where he met Pete Simmons, lunging from the other side. Their bodies smashed together and Simmons' feet left the floor and he sat down hard. Bert Garry laughed.

Simmons came off the floor with a lunge. "Laughin' at me, cowhand?"

"I reckon. You looked almighty funny, fallin' like that. I always heard a timber beast was fast on his feet."

"I'm fast enough on mine." Simmons stepped closer. "I can tear down your meat-house, cowboy."

Several other lumberjacks had moved in, forming a tight ring around the two. Shorty Jones dropped his hand to his gun, but a lumberjack nailed his wrist with a huge hand.

Shorty's only idea had been to back them off so they could walk out unmolested, but this he could never have explained. He jerked his wrist free and swung hard. And in the same instant three men swung on him. The battle was short, desperate, futile. Outnumbered four to one, the two B-Bar men were beaten brutally, then thrown into the street. They hit hard and rolled over. Bert Garry came up, choking on blood and dust, almost in tears. With a lunge he started for the door.

"Bert!" Shorty yelled. "Wait!"

Garry went through the door with a lunge and the first man he saw was Pious Pete Simmons. He swung from the hip and the blow caught the surprised lumberjack in the mouth and knocked him sprawling. Bert Garry had lost all reason. Set upon by total strangers, for what reason he had no idea, he had been beaten unfairly by a crowd of men. Now he thought of nothing but getting a little of his own back and he went into the fray with a rush.

As Simmons went down another jack sprang at Bert but, battered as he was, Garry was set and he knocked the man rolling under a table. Then he grabbed chair and waded into the crowd.

There could be but one end to such a battle, and Simmons, beside himself with fury, came off the floor and sprang on Garry's back. Out in the street Shorty Jones staggered to his feet. One arm hung useless and his eyes were closed to mere slits, but he started for the door.

He burst through the door just in time to hear an agonized scream and to see Simmons jump high in the air and come down, calks and all, on Bert Garry's face!

The cowhand screamed and tried to get up. Brutally, Simmons kicked him. Wat Williams grabbed Simmons. "Pete! Stop it! You'll kill the kid!"

Shorty dropped beside Garry. The boy's face was a mask of blood and he breathed with great gasps.

The lumberjacks had vanished, and Shorty Jones looked up to see Pious Pete Simmons leaving through the front door. "I'll see you!" The puncher was hoarse with anger. "I'll see you again!"

Wat Williams dropped on his knees beside the boy. "We'd better get this kid to the doctor. Simmons jumped on his belly, too."

"I'll get Doc McClean!" the bartender said, ducking out the door into the street.

Jones put his folded jacket under Garry's head, then looked up at Williams.

"What's this all about?"

"You don't know?" Williams sat back on his heels. "You ride for the B-Bar?"

"Sure. But we just rode in from Santa Fe. We never heard of no trouble."

Williams explained, then added, "This eye I got. Your boss gave it to me."

"Fightin's one thing. This here's another." Shorty Jones looked up at Williams and his eyes were utterly cold. "Tell Simmons to start packin' a gun. I'm goin' to kill him."

Wat Williams was silent. For the first time he was beginning to see what they had encountered. They had been in fights before, but they fought to win and did win. Simmons was not of his stripe, but Simmons had been the front man for a lot of their trouble. Now Williams could see they had stepped into a world not of lumber camps, but a world of guns and gunfighters.

When Bert Garry was safely bedded down in Doc McClean's home, Shorty crawled stiffly into the saddle and started for the B-Bar. His jaw was swelling and he was discovering bruises he had not known he had, but he knew he must get through to the ranch. Clay Bell would want to know about this.

Simmons was pulling off his boots when Wat Williams

found him. He was showing the bloody calks to the other lumberjacks. "We taught 'em!" he chuckled. "I sure greased the skids under that cow nurse!"

"We should have got the other one," Duval said.

Williams liked neither man. Some of it was in his tone when he spoke. "That's right. Now you've played hell."

They looked up at him. "The other one told me to tell you to start packin' a gun."

Simmons blinked. Slowly he put a boot down on the floor. "What would I want with a gun?"

"He said he would kill you on sight."

Simmons touched his tongue to his lips. A brutal thug, used to barroom brawls and sluggings, guns were something out of his consideration. A beating in an alley . . . a lead pipe or a cant-hook, but a gun? He drew off his other boot amid absolute silence.

Within a matter of hours the story of the fight in the Tinker House was told in every bunkhouse and prospect hole within fifty miles. Many men knew or had heard of Jud Devitt, and knew the thugs that made up his crew, men chosen as much for their ability to maim and destroy as for their ability in the timber.

Noble Wheeler heard the story with satisfaction. In this fight, as a not too innocent bystander, he stood to win no matter who lost. Knowing the way of war, he realized both sides would lose in the end. And that, he decided as he rubbed fat hands together, was exactly as he wanted it.

Morning dawned bright and clear, giving promise of a hot day. Lumberjacks this morning did not walk singly but in tight bunches of four or five men. That they held the town was obvious. There were thirty of them and all carried clubs.

The townspeople walked warily, doing their buying and hurrying off the street. Everyone waited to see what Clay Bell would do. From his big chair on the veranda of the Tinker House, Sam Tinker studied the groups of lumberjacks thoughtfully, and without pleasure.

It was going to be hot. Sam Tinker scowled and

scratched the back of his neck. This was his town. He started it, he built it. And now he did not like what was happening. He found himself looking more and more toward Emigrant Gap, and waiting.

The day moved on with no sign of anyone from the B-Bar. The lumberjacks drank in the saloons, swaggered about town and traded coarse talk. Yet there was growing uneasiness. They had always won with Jud Devitt, and they were sure they would win again, but Shorty Jones' warning to Simmons had left its effect.

Jud Devitt, accompanied by Williams and Duval, had left town before daylight, headed for The Notch. It was a long and rugged ride over rough country. They were compelled to circle widely because The Notch lay almost directly opposite the town and across the mountains.

Before leaving town Devitt had sent three wires, one to Washington, one to the state capital, and one to the county seat. He would have the law on his side. Devitt was not worried about Garry, and whether the cowhand lived or died, he did not care. His death could always be passed off as a barroom brawl. But a lot could be done with that threat to kill.

Noble Wheeler had also been active. A year before Montana Brown had been implicated in a shooting at Weaver. Brown had undoubtedly been in the right, so the shooting had been passed over and forgotten. Now Wheeler started the wheels turning to reopen the case and have Brown arrested. That the man would be acquitted was unimportant. He would be out of action during the coming battle.

He sat back in his musty office in the bank and chuckled as he considered the situation. It was going his way—he could not lose.

CHAPTER 7

CLAY BELL received Shorty's report in silence. The stocky cowhand had come immediately to the ranch house and he was still caked with dried blood and his eyes swollen almost shut. His wrist, although not broken, was badly injured and the arm all but useless. Of the twelve men on whom Clay counted, two were now out of action.

The hands crowded in. "What's next, Boss?" Montana was ready for trouble. "Do we go to town?"

"No."

He sat very quiet, listening to their angry protests until they quieted. He had expected trouble, but not this soon, and it gave him a new measure of Jud Devitt. The man was not one to waste time, nor to stop at killing.

"Hold it!" He lifted a hand. "The only way we can take care of this is to win the fight. If we lose now he will hound down every last one of us. Now we have him stopped here. What's his next move?"

"The Notch. He'll try The Notch."

"You're right, Hank, and I think he'll try it today. Now don't think I wouldn't like to go down to Tinker, but don't you believe he isn't expecting it. He's got at least thirty men in town. If we took everybody we'd still be outnumbered and we'd have to leave this place unguarded."

Montana Brown swore softly. "All right. What do we do? Sit on our hands?"

"We stand pat. We watch the Gap and The Notch."

When they were gone, Clay got to his feet. "Hank, I'm going to town myself."

"Alone?"

"I want to see Wheeler. If we're going to have a war we'll need money."

When Hank followed the others, Clay walked to the edge of the veranda and looked down the valley. Devitt's

48

men and teams were still waiting, just beyond the white marker.

Hank Rooney, Coffin, and Shorty would remain at the Gap. Shorty could still use his left hand, if need be.

Montana Brown and Rush Jackson had returned to The Notch. Two men could easily defend either place. Other hands were scouting or on lookout.

Point by point he considered the situation, trying to overlook nothing. There had been no word from Tibbott. That might mean nothing, and it might mean everything. Jud Devitt must have taken care to have a man in Washington, to try to get a grant of land or the right to log off Deep Creek. If he got such a right, a U.S. Marshal would enforce it.

All he could do now was sit tight and wait for Devitt to move. But he would need money. And he should hire more riders. He thought of Harvey and Kilburn, then dismissed the thought. The men were too bloody, had too many killings behind them. If it came to a court battle, the hiring of such men would stand against him.

Mounting the palouse, he took the trail to Deep Creek. It was cool and still and the spotted horse walked swiftly through the tall grass under the stately columns of the Douglas fir. They grew straight and tall, and the thought of seeing them cut gave him a pang. The destruction of such trees left nothing but desolation behind, for trees like that would take years to grow again; and so they would never grow again, for man in his haste would not allow them the years they would need to become so magnificent.

The grass rustled with the movement of the horse's hoofs. Far away an eagle cried, and somewhere he could hear water falling. The sound of wind in the tree tops was like the rushing of a distant train.

On his left Piety Mountain lifted, shouldering brutally against the sky. There were still streaks of snow in the cracks and hollow places where the sun had not yet reached. Here, away from the heat of the flatlands, it was utterly still, cool, restful.

Without thinking, he had turned his horse toward the

headwaters of Deep Creek and the old Bullwinkle claim. There, too, was the ghost town of Cave Creek, deserted by all but pack rats and owls. Beyond the town, and beyond Quartz Mountain, was an old burro trail that would take him into Tinkersville from the opposite end of town.

Pausing at Cave Creek to water the palouse, he changed his plans. He would not slip quietly in and out of town. He would give them a treat. He would go right down the main drag in full sight of everyone. He would show them clearly where he stood, and that Devitt inspired him with no fear.

While the palouse rested, he wandered among the dilapidated buildings of the ghost town. Grass grew high in the streets and a pine had forced its way up through the porch of the saloon and stood twenty feet high. Some roofs had fallen in; most of the buildings were near collapse. Returning to his horse, he mounted and took to the burro trail.

It was no trail for the inexperienced. Steep, and in places almost washed away by torrential rains, it required a good mountain horse to descend it. Reaching the bottom, he hesitated long enough for a prolonged survey of the flatlands, then took to a wash and after that skirted hills to keep himself under cover.

At the head of the street he slowed his horse to a walk and, his right hand resting on his thigh, he walked it down the street, sitting straight in the saddle.

It was midafternoon and the sun lay like a curse upon the town. Clusters of men in laced boots, each with a club, stood stock-still and watched him come. On the steps of the Tinker House, Bob Tripp took his pipe from his mouth and stared. Old Sam Tinker chuckled fatly, and rubbed his palm on the polished arm of his chair.

Clay rode on through town until he drew up before Doc McClean's adobe.

McClean met him at the door. He was a tall old man with a shock of white hair and a mustache. "Clay! Glad you came in. This boy's in bad shape."

Garry was unconscious and breathing hoarsely. His face

was bandaged, but the little Bell could see was a ghastly gray. Clay put his hand on the cowboy's shoulder.

"It's all right, Bert," he said gently. "We're with you, all the way!"

As though he had sensed the touch or heard the low voice, the young rider stirred and turned his head.

Outside in the living room, McClean shook his head. "I can't say," he replied to Clay's question. "The boy's in mighty bad shape. He'll lose the sight of one eye and carry the scars to his dying day, but that's not the worst of it. He has five broken ribs and one punctured a lung. I'm doing what I can."

They talked a little longer, but at the door Doc McClean put a hand on Clay's arm. "Boy, I've got to tell you this. Somebody dug up that old killing of Monty's and they're getting out a warrant."

Devitt could not have known that without being tipped off. This was another evidence that he had local advice or aid.

"Take care of Garry, Doc. And don't let him worry. We'll make out."

Down the sunlit street stood dark groups of men, looking up the street toward him. The sun was hot and the air heavy with that sultry heat that so often precedes a storm.

They were waiting for him down there. Wryly, he considered the situation. It would solve a lot of problems for Devitt if he were put out of business, yet it was not in him to duck an issue, and the issue lay right down there among those gatherings of men.

If they should gang him, not a hand would be lifted in his aid, unless it was that of old Sam Tinker. He built a smoke, taking his time. At that, Tinker, old as he was, might be the best man in town.

First, he must talk to Noble Wheeler. He stepped into the saddle, and only then lighted his cigarette. He drew deep on the smoke and it tasted good. Mentally, he smiled at himself. He could feel that old steadiness inside him, that queer sort of calm he always felt when going into trouble. And he had known a lot of trouble. Perhaps more than any one of those men. Perhaps more than any dozen. It had not been like this that first day when the Comanches hit the wagon train when he was a youngster. Yet he had scored a hit with his first shot.

He walked his horse the fifty yards to the bank, the only moving thing along the street. He felt sweat trickle down his cheeks, felt the good feel of the horse between his knees, saw without turning his head the dark groups of men, one of them before the bank.

One of these men had a swollen jaw. It was Pete Simmons. Simmons stood almost in the doorway, but Clay could step around him. He had no intention of doing so. He stepped down from the horse and walked straight at Simmons, looking straight ahead. Simmons did not move.

Bell walked on and Simmons held his ground until with one more step he would have walked right into him, and then Simmons gave ground. Bell went on into the bank.

Noble Wheeler looked up from his desk, his fat face wreathed in smiles.

"Howdy, Clay! Glad to see you!"

Bell dropped into a chair and shoved his hat back on his head. Wheeler's vest was spotted and soiled, his cheeks unshaven.

The little office smelled musty and old, as if long unaired. The sunlight made a small rectangle of light upon the floor, and glinted from the brass cuspidor.

"Noble, I'm going to need some money to see me through."

Wheeler traced a design upon his desk with a stub of pencil. "You owe me a good bit, Clay," he said ponderously. "I'd like to help, but the way I see it, with Devitt taking your best range—"

"He isn't taking it."

Wheeler looked up out of his pale eyes. "Folks think he'll get it, Clay. He's got money and political influence. To tell you the truth, Clay, the bank can't risk it. Right now you're a mighty unsafe risk."

Clay drew thoughtfully on his cigarette. Now that it had come, he realized he had more than half expected just this. He could not pay his hands without money, and he owed Kesterson over at the store. Kesterson was friendly, but a sharp businessman.

"Wheeler," he protested quietly, "I'll pay every cent, you know that. We'll win—we simply can't lose. He can't even get on the plateau."

"You sure?"

"He knows I own the Gap. I also own The Notch." Clay took off his hat and turned it in his hands. "Sooner or later this was bound to come. I made sure my range was protected, and you can be sure that I thought of everything."

Noble Wheeler shifted his heavy body. So he owned The Notch? Wheeler wanted to ask a question, but decided against it. He had his own ambitions in regard to Deep Creek, but they must wait. But he was surprised and irritated that Bell had shown the forethought to buy those two pieces and so control fifty thousand acres of range.

The thought worried him. What else did Bell know? Or would he guess?

"I'd like to help you," he said, putting on a helpless air, "but money is tight and I've got some loans coming due. Sorry, Clay."

At the store, Kesterson filled his order without comment. As he stacked the groceries he started to speak, hesitated, and said nothing.

Once more in the saddle, Clay headed for the station. Behind him a lumberjack yelled, "Better grab a train while you're able, cowhand!"

Somebody else gave vent to a raucous yell, and it was followed by jeers and catcalls. Clay rode steadily on, his face a mask. When he dismounted at the station he noticed that the lumberjacks were bunching together and following.

He went into the station with rapid strides. "Jim! Bell. Can I talk to you?"

Jim Narrows rolled the curtain away from the wicket and looked out. "Howdy, Clay. What can I do for you?"

"Get me about a dozen cars. I want to ship cattle."

Narrows was embarrassed. "Sorry, Clay. I can't get 'em." He leaned toward Bell. "Betwixt you an' me, we got orders

to ship no cattle for you. Comes from higher up. Looks
like they're fishin' for that lumber contract."

"I see . . . thanks, Jim."

He hesitated, staring out the door. So they had blocked
him there, too. Devitt thought of everything. The circle
was drawing tighter.

"Clay."

He turned back to Narrows.

"There was a wire sent about Monty Brown."

"Devitt?"

"No." Narrows leaned closer. "It was Wheeler."

Clay Bell stared at the station master. "Wheeler sent
it?"

"His very own self."

Bell turned away. "Thanks, Jim. Do you a favor some
day."

He walked outside and stopped abruptly. One of the
lumberjacks had untied the palouse and mounted it, and
a dozen others made a tight cordon between himself and
the horse. They stood staring at him and grinning. He
recognized the situation and understood it. Here was real
trouble.

They were out to get him now. If he drew a gun he
might kill one man, but he could not kill them all. The
men he faced knew that and were prepared to gamble. A
flicker of movement caught the tail of his eye, a movement from the open door of a barn hayloft.

The flicker of movement had been sunlight on a rifle
barrel.

CHAPTER 8

CLAY BELL took his time. He was a tall, serene man at this moment, showing no sign of nerves or hesitation, merely a man studying a situation and seeking a way out. At least twenty of the burly lumberjacks stood around. A few showed malice, some merely rough good humor, but all were waiting to see what he would do.

His eyes strayed down the street, flickering past the loft door where he had detected movement. There was nothing to be seen, but he was not fooled. The unknown marksman was in position and ready. The shot had to come at the right time, when its origin would not be obvious.

This was an old story to Clay. He dropped his cigarette into the dust and shifted his position slightly. It put a man between himself and that loft door.

He glanced at the appalousa, restive under the strange rider, then at the men around him.

"You boys sure like to gang up on a man, don't you?" He drawled his words, smiling a little, his manner casual. "What's the matter? Afraid to fight one man at a time?"

A big man shouldered his way to the front of the crowd. "I'll fight you, now or—"

Clay's fist smashed his lips even as he spoke. Then he crossed a right and the thud of his fist was like the butt end of an axe striking a log. The lumberjack fell flat on his face and instantly, Bell whistled.

The appalousa whirled and lunged through the crowd toward Bell, scattering lumberjacks in every direction. The rider sawed on the bit, and the palouse tossed his head, then duck it between his legs and kicked out wickedly. He took a stiff-legged hop and ducked his head again and the jack went over his head into the dirt.

As the horse spun, Bell grabbed the pommel and swung to the saddle, shucking his Colt as his toe kicked into the

55

stirrup. He tilted it and blasted a shot at the loft door even as the rifle spoke. He heard the whip of the bullet past his ear, but his own bullet had scored. The man in the loft let go his rifle and lunged to his feet, holding his wounded arm. Bell fired again, and the man leaned far out from the door and then hit the dust of the street on his face, falling like a sack of meal.

Clay Bell put his horse into the street and went down the main drag at a pounding run. A lumberjack ran from the Tinker House to see what had happened and Bell threw a shot into the planks at his feet. The man dove at the door, clawing for the latch.

Then Bell was outside of town and his horse was running free. The last thing he saw as he went out of town on a hard gallop was Colleen Riley. She had come out on the upstairs porch of the hotel and stared after him.

A half-mile out of town he slowed the horse to a canter, then to a walk.

Now the full force of those arrayed against him was making itself felt. Noble Wheeler was without doubt the man behind Devitt, the source of Devitt's information, and perhaps the reason why he had chosen to get his timber from the Deep Creek forest.

No loan was to be had and he could ship no cattle. He was broke, flat broke.

He held the only two known routes into Deep Creek, but the enemy held the whip hand. Kesterson might continue to sell him supplies but it would mean a gun battle to get them. He was encircled and they could draw the noose tighter. It was small consolation that they could scarcely starve him out as long as he had beef.

One man was dead. Bell knew his own shooting well enough to know he had killed the unknown dry-gulcher who fired from the loft door.

His first shot had disarmed the man, his second had killed him. This was war—war to the death. Devitt had made that obvious in the brutal attack on Garry and Jones. And now in this attempt to kill him from ambush. Bell could have spared the man in the loft, but only to give him another chance. And in this battle there were to be no second chances for anyone.

Jud Devitt had prepared his ground well, and it was equally obvious that he intended to use the forces of the law whenever possible. The old shooting in which Montana Brown had engaged had long ago been dropped without a charge being filed. No jury would convict him now, but he could be arrested and held for trial, and to resist arrest would be to play right into Devitt's hands. Clay had no doubt the warrant would be served by a posse made up of Devitt's own men.

Drawing up at the crest of a low hill, he scanned his back trail. It was growing late, and the sun was already behind the mountain. The softness of desert evening was settling over the mesquite country, and he sat his horse a minute, studying the terrain with a careful eye. At no time would he be safe, but there was nothing on the trail, no dust, no movement.

The palouse, restless for home, moved off of his own volition, and Clay let him go. The air was cooler now with the sudden coolness of a desert sundown. The pastels of evening gathered in changing color along the far off hills. The sky held a lone star, and somewhere a coyote yapped shrilly.

Before him the dark mass of the mountain loomed, bare rock, tufted with vegetation in the draws and canyons, and showing the darkness of forest on its higher slopes. A distant sound, foreign to the evening, caught his ears; he drew up sharply against the black of a clump of brush, listening.

The night was silent . . . no sound . . . only cool air, refreshing as a drink of clear, cold water. He drew it deep into his lungs, touched with the faint scent of sage. The palouse moved on, and slowly his hand came away from his gun butt.

Each clump of mesquite or juniper now was a spot of darkness. The floor of the desert was gray . . . more stars blossomed in the clear field of the sky. His horse walked on, and suddenly, there was a flicker of darker shadow among the mesquite clumps and metal clicked.

Clay threw himself flat along the horse just as something struck him a wicked blow on the shoulder. He grabbed wildly at the saddle horn and clutched it with a drowning man's grip. There was another shot, and he was struck again, and he seemed to go tumbling forward, over and over into soft, velvety darkness, but his fingers clung to the one real thing in all this nightmare . . . the saddle horn. With all his will, his fingers shut down on it and held.

Through a heaving, roaring blackness he felt himself plunging ahead. Behind him there was another sharp, splitting crack . . . then no other sound.

Clay Bell fought his way back to consciousness into the sunlight. He lay flat on his back, half under a tree, and the sky beyond the tree was blue and flecked with fleecy clouds. He could hear his horse cropping grass near by, and he lay very still, afraid to move, trying to locate himself.

He had been to Tinkersville. That much was clear. There had been trouble there, but he'd ridden safely from the town. He scowled over that, puzzling at what else might have happened and where he might be now.

Evening . . . it had been cool and pleasant . . . he had been riding. Then it all came back, clear and sharp. He had been ambushed, dry-gulched. Yet how could that be? The burro trail toward which he had been headed was unknown in the valley, and it was unlikely that any of Jud Devitt's crew could have happened upon it.

Now pain made itself felt. It was his right shoulder. He rolled over carefully, using his left hand, pushing up to a sitting position. Carefully, turning his head on a stiff neck, he looked around.

He was among the ghost buildings of Cave Creek. Somehow his will must have kept his grip on that saddle horn until he reached here. Assurance of safety must have let his subconscious relax that death grip, and he had fallen.

His mouth and throat were parched and there was no strength in him. Using his left hand, he pulled himself the dozen yards to the mountain stream and drank deep. Then, working with his left hand, he ripped the shirt over his wounds. Two bullets had hit him. One had skidded off the shoulder muscle, ripping the deltoid. This wound was scarcely more than a graze. The other had gone through his shoulder below the collarbone.

Carefully, not to start the bleeding again, he bathed both wounds in cold water. It was a slow, painstaking job, and when it was finished he lay back on the grass, panting heavily. His thoughts were muggy and he could not seem to bring them to any focus. Undoubtedly he had lost much blood. For a long while he lay on his back staring up at the sky.

A distant sound of firing brought him out of it. He struggled to his feet and started toward the palouse, but his weakness was too great. Something hooked over his boot toe and he fell, sprawling upon the ground.

When his eyes opened again it was sunset and the air was cool. He lay there against the grass, his shoulder on fire and his head humming. A long time later, while he was listening to the water running over the stones, he heard in his memory the sound of firing. Clay lifted his head to listen, but heard no sound. He remembered then that he heard the firing hours ago, before noon.

He lay back upon the grass. There had been trouble and he had not been there to help. He rolled over and got to his knees, crawling again to the stream where he could drink long and deep of the cold water. His thirst seemed without end . . . and he remembered from somewhere that thirst usually accompanied loss of blood

The memory of those shots blasting out of the darkness returned. Probably not Jud Devitt . . . how could the contractor have known of the old trail? But there was no reason for anyone being near this point unless to wait for him. Who in town would know that he used this trail? Or that the trail existed?

His head throbbed heavily and his shoulder flamed, but he sat up and tried to assay his position. Nothing in the situation was favorable except that he was alive. He had no way of knowing what had happened at the Gap, nor at The Notch. The shooting had to come from the latter place—he was still too far to hear firing from Emigrant Gap.

In his present condition he was no good to anyone. On the other hand, there was not a chance in a million that anyone would ride this way unless one of his own men came looking for him. The first thing would be to check his weapons to make sure he was prepared to defend himself, get the saddle off the palouse, and to dress his wounds, somehow.

He was on the bank of the stream with the nearest building not twenty yards off. It was the sagging frame structure of what had, by the faded sign, once been the town's saloon. Across the street was an assay office, and farther down were other buildings, all of frame or log construction.

Behind a dugout was a field of maize, now gone wild. It was only a few yards distant. On his second try Clay managed to get to his feet, and behind the saloon he found an old pickle jar. He dipped water, built a small fire of dry sticks from around the saloon, and soon had the water boiling. From the long abandoned field he got some maize and, having pounded it to fragments, made a poultice to put on his wounded shoulder after he had bathed it in hot water.

It was a slow process, and he stopped many times to rest. Luckily, the bullet had gone on through his shoulder. When the wound had been bathed and the poultice tied on, he got to the palouse and slipped off the saddle and bridle, then picketed the horse on the grass near the stream.

For himself he found a hollow inside the foundation of a ruined building and settled down with the sun to warm his bones. He awakened with a start and glanced quickly at the sun. He must have slept at least two hours. He made his way to the stream and drank again.

Clay seated himself and stared at the water. His face was hot and his mouth dry. He bathed the wound again and changed the poultice. Aware of his hunger, he ate jerked beef from his saddlebag, then gathered his blanket around him and lay on the ground.

His head throbbed with slow, heavy throbs, and a slow fire burned in the injured shoulder. He kept flexing his fingers, frightened of stiffness, knowing the danger that could come to him now, in this hour of trial, if he failed in gun skill.

Several times he lost consciousness, whether in sleep or weakness he did not know. Shadows seemed to peer at him from the darkness under the trees and he stared up at the wide sky, caught in some vague enchantment by a drifting cloud which he watched through long, intent minutes. A cricket chirped . . . cicadas sang in the hot, lazy afternoon. He lay quiet and, after a while, lulled by the heat, the crickets, and the stream, he slept.

He awakened in complete darkness. Night had come while he slept and with it a penetrating chill from off the high peaks. His fever had left him and he was shaking with chill, despite the blanket. He crawled to the stream and drank. The water was cold, but it went down his throat like some crystalline elixir, giving him strength and new life. He lay back after he had finished drinking and huddled in his blankets. His head throbbed and his shoulder held a small pulsating beat.

Wind stirred in the crests of the pines and off in the blackness of the forest a tree branch scraped. From the ghostly buildings came faint, creaking sounds. A loose shutter swayed on rusty hinges, there was a scurrying of tiny feet, and something small and animate stirred the tall grass. The moon was rising just above the ridge and it stretched long shadows behind the buildings, and turned the rank grass of the street into a silver flowing stream.

He had to move . . . His mind told him that he must move but his muscles did not respond. He huddled closer in his blankets and watched the moon rise until it swung free above the black, serrated ridge. The wide black eyes of glassless windows peered at him. He had to move. He must get up. He must get a saddle on his horse. He must get back. They would believe him dead. They would retaliate and men would be killed.

He rolled over and got to his knees. Near by his horse cropped grass and he went to it and led it to the saddle.

He stooped, after the blanket was in place and free of wrinkles, and grasped the heavy stock saddle. He waited, mustering strength, then swung it free and to the horse's back.

Exhausted by the effort, he leaned against the horse and counted the heavy throbs in his skull. Then he got the bridle on and thrust his rifle back in the boot. Grasping the pommel, he pulled himself into the saddle, still clutching the blankets around his shoulders.

The Notch was closest—he would go there. There was no antidote for the throbbing pain in his shoulder, but he had never been a man who spared himself. Wounds were not new to him and he had seen many a bullet wound treated by pushing a silk handkerchief through the hole with a stick, and a little medicine dabbed on, of whatever kind was available.

A kindly man with others, he could be harsh with himself, and wounded or not he had no right to sit here when men were risking their lives to protect his property. He almost forgot his pain, shaken as he was by a deep-seated anger.

And that very anger frightened him. Clay Bell knew himself, and he was quiet partly to cover what lay under the surface. He was actually a man of violent and explosive temper, carefully guarded against and usually controlled; but occasionally, under exceptional strain, he had given way to outbursts of berserk fury. He was always better when thinking for others . . . he must get back to them and their sobering influence.

Reaching Deep Creek, he waded the horse through the stream and up the bank. The fever was on him again now, and his shoulder, aroused by handling the heavy saddle, was a steady beat of agony. No longer conscious of the coolness and the night, he was shaking with pain and with fury.

He had asked for none of this. He had lived quietly here, far from the old trails, the gun trails, the kill-hungry men he had known. He had built carefully here, planning for the future. Now the greed of one man could destroy all that, wreck lives and ruin the health of a pleasant young cowhand who bothered no one.

Bert Garry lay minus an eye and scarred for life, perhaps soon to die, because of the ruthless brutality of that one man.

And someone lying in ambush had shot Clay himself, had tried to kill him.

Branches slapped at his shoulders and his head felt heavy. There was sickness on him, and the heaviness of pain, and the moon seemed vague in the wide sky. The trees loomed right and left and all around him. He sat in the saddle like a drunken man, and like a drunken man there throbbed in his brain only the thought of what had been done and a driving urge to fight, to smash, to kill . . . .

Suddenly he felt the mustang's muscles tighten and saw its ears come up. Instinct snapped him to himself, his long living with danger alerting him now. He drew up, listening.

A moment passed when only the stream rustled behind him . . . and then he smelled woodsmoke, and heard voices.

They were strange voices, and none of his men would be here, close to The Notch, yet away from it.

His mouth felt dry and something rose up inside of him. So they had broken through. Brown and Jackson might have been killed. . . . Red rage began to take him and he felt his body begin to tremble.

A stick cracked and someone said, "Pete Simmons took their heart out when he jumped the Garry kid. This fight's over."

Inside him something welled up and burst. He dropped his hand to his left gun and he yelled, a wild rebel yell torn with pain and fury. And then he slapped spurs to the horse and leaped him through the brush into the firelight.

Startled lumberjacks came to their feet, eyes wild. One man grabbed at a rifle, but Bell's gun smashed a shot and the man screamed, dropping the rifle to grab a broken shoulder. A bullet smashed the coffee pot, another ripped at the bed of the fire, scattering sparks and embers. He

was across the camp and gone into darkness, his gun stabbing flame.

And then he wheeled, swaying in the saddle, his face
hard and savage. Deliberately he lifted the gun and proceeded to put a hole in everything in sight.

Reloading, he smashed the frying pan, emptied the
water bucket, smashed a rifle stock, and burned the ribs of
a man scrambling for a gun.

Sitting his horse, he filled his gun again. Then he walked
his horse back to the edge of camp.

CHAPTER 9

THERE WAS no one in sight. He drew up, then swung his horse and rode toward The Notch. They would have someone on guard there, and he must find out what had happened to his men.

His shoulder was leaping with pain, adding to his bitter savagery. But at this moment he welcomed the pain, for it was an added incentive.

He came up to the three men guarding The Notch before they heard him. He had come upon them over the pine needles where his horse made no sound. He saw them with the firelight on their faces, heard their laughter, and smelled the smoke of their fire, and the fine smell of coffee.

He came out of the shadows like a ghost and drew up, and Tripp looked around. Shocked, he came to his feet.

Clay Bell sat hunched in the saddle, his face a gray mask of savagery, his shoulder and shirt blood-stained, his eyes wild from the throbbing in his skull and the solid agony from his wound.

In his left hand he held a negligent Colt. "Take off your boots."

He did not seem to lift his voice yet it boomed hollowly against the black walled cliffs. Bob Tripp stared at him, his mouth opening and closing.

"Take 'em off!" He punctuated the order with a bullet into the fire.

"What's the idea?" Tripp demanded, fighting for time.

"Tripp," Bell's voice was dangerously calm, "take off your boots or I'll break both your knees."

Tripp saw the wildness in Bell's eyes. He backed up abruptly and almost fell into a sitting position. There was insanity in this, but . . . When all three had their boots off they looked up at Bell.

"Start for town."

"What?" Tripp's face turned sickly. "By the Lord, Bell, you—!"

"Start moving, Tripp, or you can die right here. Your boys stomped Garry, they've tried to kill me. Now start going or you can lie in a pile, right here."

There was crashing in the brush and then Duval burst through, followed by the others from the upper camp. "Tripp!" Duval was bawling the words as he ran. "That Bell, he—"

They had rifles. Clay Bell swung his gun. "Drop them!"

A lean redhead started to swing his rifle to shooting position and Clay Bell's gun bucked. The red-headed man turned half around and dropped, clutching a smashed shoulder.

"You, too. Off with your boots!"

Lining up the nine men in the two groups, he started them for town, moving them down the rocky Notch Trail in their sock feet.

He did not let them leave alone. A few yards behind, he followed, keeping them hustling. The socks tore, they wore out on the lava of the trail, their feet became bloody. When they reached the desert he started them well away from the shelter and shade of the hills, then let them go.

"You came hunting it," he said, "now see how you like it. Come back if you want . . . I'll be ready."

He was swaying from weariness, scarcely capable of keeping his eyes open. He turned the appalousa then and started at a canter toward the home ranch. His mind was a blur. Had anyone seen him then he would have been a sitting duck. His shoulder throbbed, his head felt like a half-filled bucket in which the blood slopped from side to side. He muttered and talked, but the palouse was going home now, and he kept moving.

Hank Rooney ran to meet him. "Boss! We figured you was dead!"

He clung to the pommel. "Sheriff been here? After Brown?"

Rooney was puzzled. "The sheriff? No—ain't seen him. What's wrong with Brown?"

Tripp had managed to get some of his men up over

The Notch on foot. They had come down on Brown and
Jackson from behind and driven both men off. Bell ordered the two men back to The Notch. This time they
would hole up in a cave that offered good cover and an
almost impregnable position.

Hank Rooney stripped off Clay's shirt and worked over
his shoulder. Long before he had finished cleansing the
wound and treating it, Clay was asleep.

Two quiet days passed, and nothing happened. Shorty
Jones nursed his injured wrist and grew steadily more ugly
and morose. Whether Bert Garry was alive or dead no
one had any idea.

Clay Bell slept, awoke to scout around the ranch, ate
and slept again. There was no move from the lumberjacks
beyond the white stone. They sat still, waiting, nobody
knew for what.

Angry at their enforced idleness, and undoubtedly angry
at what had happened at The Notch, they yelled at the
guards from time to time, trying to start trouble. One
came halfway up the trail, in a swaggering walk. When
he came a step too far, Hank Rooney dusted his toes with
a bullet and he wheeled and ran. More bullets helped him
on his way.

There was no word from Hardy Tibbott. More days
went slowly by. Bell worked over his accounts, rode twice
to The Notch. His wounds were on the mend and he felt
better. He could use his right hand, but not without pain
and discomfort.

Bill Coffin checked the cows on his way back from
Piety. "Fattenin', Boss. Be good beef there, mighty soon."

Nothing was reported from The Notch. Devitt had
made no further attempt on that side.

Restlessly, the B-Bar riders patrolled the limits of their
range. The ring of hills around the Deep Creek area made
their problem relatively easy, for much of it was abrupt
faces of rock or steep, rugged slopes over which a man
might scramble with hand and foot, but where no wheeled
vehicle or even a horse might be taken.

The B-Bar riders rode with their rifles across their sad-

dle-bows, and in the mind of each man was a picture of
Bert Garry with his scarred face and lost eye, laboring to
breathe with a punctured lung.

Jud Devitt entered the musty office where Noble
Wheeler sat behind his desk and dropped into a chair. He
looked smug and pleased this morning. He was freshly
shaved, and Wheeler caught a whiff of shaving lotion.
Devitt bit the end from a black cigar and leaned back. For
the first time since his meeting with Bell in the street, he
felt that the situation was completely in hand.

"We've got him, Noble. Judge Riley's issuing an injunction that will force Bell to allow free passage over
the old stage route until the case can come to trial." He
chuckled. "By that time it won't matter. We'll have logged
off that piece and have the logs cut into ties."

"That injunction—who will enforce it?"

"A Deputy United States Marshal we'll have appointed."

"You namin' him?"

"Who else?"

Devitt smoked quietly for several minutes, considering
the situation. Suddenly a thought occurred to him.
"Wheeler, who is Hardy Tibbott?"

Noble Wheeler turned his face to Devitt. He was alert,
suddenly anxious. "He's a lawyer. An able man. Knows
folks."

"He's in Washington, trying to get a permanent grazing
right for Bell."

Noble Wheeler came around sharply in his chair. His
heavy face was shadowed with worry. "I should have
guessed it! He's liable to trouble us!"

"Chase will handle that end." Devitt had been interested, but he was not worried.

Wheeler muttered and fumed, and Devitt stared down
at the back of his hands, wishing he had an hour alone
in this office. There might be some clue as to what the
banker planned. He dared not even hint at the subject,
for Wheeler was shrewd. Whatever it was he had in mind,
he would do no talking.

It was time for some action now. When the marshal was

appointed he would ride to Emigrant Gap and Bell would be forced to give right-of-way through to Deep Creek. It had shaped up like a battle, and that move would end it.

Or would it? Irritably, Jud Devitt realized that it was no certainty. Clay Bell was a man who could plan as well as fight. There was, too, a noticeable lack of eagerness among some of the men. The Bell who had attacked them at The Notch had put the fear of God into them.

He glanced out of the bank window and saw a man standing in the door of the Homestake Saloon. He was a tall man, lean-bodied and tough, with black hair that looked like a skull cap on his head. This was Stag Harvey.

It might come to that. Devitt had seen the other one, too. Jack Kilburn was a short, thick-set man with a round, plump face. He looked like anything but a killer. Yet they waited as if they knew their time was coming.

Queer places a man's ambition got him to. He had never liked western towns . . . the hotels and polish of the East, that was like it. Even San Francisco or New Orleans, but not these ramshackle towns on the edge of nowhere at all.

Here he sat in this musty, unaired bank office, looking across the street at a man who killed for hire. He dropped his hands to his knees. Time to be moving.

"Tibbott can be a trouble," Wheeler said suddenly, "but it's Garry who worries me."

Devitt was not sure he had heard correctly. "Garry? The wounded man?"

"If that cowboy dies the B-Bar will come off Deep Creek huntin' scalps."

"Nonsense!" Devitt got to his feet. This sort of talk irritated him. There had been more of it before this, when men got together around town. He had listened to some of them talk. "There aren't enough of them to make trouble even if they dared."

Wheeler sat back in his chair. It creaked heavily. He prodded in his vest pockets for something, looked around the desk . . . then found it. A match.

He picked up his pipe and began to stoke it slowly.

"Montana Brown, Rush Jackson, Bill Coffin, Shorty Jones, and Hank Rooney? That's an army."

Despite his impatience at the talk, and his total disbelief that anything would come of it, Devitt found the thought nagging at his mind. So much so that when he met Colleen for dinner, he brought up the subject.

"You've been to see this Garry fellow. How is he?"

Colleen wore a blue gown this evening, and the color brought out the deep blue of her eyes. She lifted her eyes and looked across the table at him, a strange, searching, measuring glance.

"He is better," she admitted, "if you can call a man better who is permanently scarred and has lost one eye."

"He won't die then?" Some of his relief was in his tone.

Colleen lifted her cup. This evening, for the first time, she was less than proud of Jud Devitt. She was beginning to see him in a new light. Her father's friends in Philadelphia and Washington had spoken of him as a go-getter, a man who got things done. She was beginning to understand how he got them done.

"He will be all right if he doesn't get pneumonia. Dr. McClean says that with his bad lung he wouldn't have a chance. It's nothing short of a miracle that he has lived this long."

Devitt sensed her disapproval and turned the conversation.

Judge Riley shared some of his daughter's feelings. He looked at his food with distaste. He had accepted what amounted to orders from Devitt, and had gone along because Devitt usually had a strong case. Now he was less sure. Jud Devitt was an ambitious man, and if he had ever possessed any feelings for the men around him, those feelings had been swallowed by his ambition and confidence in his own innate rightness.

Of late, during their casual conversations, Devitt had talked at length, and Judge Riley was a good listener. With more and more disquiet he had heard Devitt express his feelings. Many of their friends would have agreed that Devitt was right. This was a growing country, an expanding country, and a man had to grow with it. If in the process he knocked over a few smaller men—well, competition was the law of growth.

Or was it? Judge Riley remembered that the Colonies had a bad time of it until they started working together. It was no different with men. There was a place for competition, but a bigger place for cooperation.

Judge Riley was a tall man, lean and quiet. His features and expression were those of the student rather than the man of action. He knew law, and adhered closely to the letter of the law, but since he had come west, here with these people of wider, more liberal view, he was beginning to feel what one of his old teachers had long ago told him. That no matter what the letter of the law said, it was of purely general application. It was the judge and his sense of justice that gave law its meaning. There were differences. All cases were not black or white—there were many shades of gray.

Two days before, buying a cigar in Kesterson's, the storekeeper had said, briefly, "Good man, Bell. Hard-working, sincere. Country needs men like that."

Kesterson gestured widely. "Most of these are drifters. When he came here nearly all of them were. Clay Bell came in here, scouted Deep Creek, put down his roots."

Judge Riley had considered that. Kesterson was a man he understood. He was like his own solid New England-Pennsylvania ancestors.

Devitt, he was beginning to feel, was a man who considered the law a tool to be used, rather than a means to justice that should be treated with respect. That night in his room the judge turned idly the pages of his Blackstone.

Men had not arrived at these principles quickly. Within the covers of this book, and of all books that dealt with the laws of men, within those covers there was a little of Hammurabi, a little of Moses, memories of Greek and Roman, of the Magna Carta, and of the first Colonists—each had contributed something. The law was a maze of many turnings, justice was the one true path through that maze . . . .

On the upper veranda of the hotel he looked off toward the mountains. Was Bell awake at this hour? Of what did he think? Did he think of justice and the rights of man?

A faint wind stirred the sage and brought its scent to the judge. What must this country have been like when Bell first came? For that matter, when Sam Tinker first settled here?

CHAPTER 10

IN THE ranch house at Emigrant Gap, Clay Bell was sitting beside his table staring at his accounts. He hated book work, and particularly when his books gave him no comfort, as tonight. To ride herd, to judge beef, to know grass land and range country—those were what he knew best.

And tonight it was worse. His shoulder itched and burned. It was healing, growing rapidly better. The rough life might not be conducive to comfort but it did build strength, and he was coming out of it rapidly. But behind and beyond the figures that stared up at him from the cheap tablet on the table, there was a shadowy figure. He had been shot at by a man who wanted to kill him.

That man could not have been Jud Devitt. He was positive, perhaps unreasonably so, of that. Devitt might try to kill him. He might even hire him killed, but it would not be by ambush. Devitt would be sure to be accused of such a killing—and Devitt, for all his ruthlessness, was not that sort of a fighter.

The fact remained that he had been shot at. By whom?

On the porch of the Tinker House sat a man who might have given him an idea, and that man was fat Sam Tinker, who whiled away his hours smoking on the porch. Smoking and observing life. Little could happen in the town that Sam did not know, and he understood more than anyone suspected.

Usually, people believe their motives and emotions are known to themselves alone, yet few things remain concealed from an intelligent observer with time to see, to consider, and to speculate. Sam Tinker, from the porch before the hotel which he owned, missed very little.

The bartender at the Tinker House was having trouble with his wife. The burly young blacksmith was flirting with Simpson's oldest daughter. Sam Tinker observed these

73

simple things and many more, watching the town named for him, with the kindly tolerance of a grandfather.

He had watched Clay Bell ride from town after his visit to the railroad station. He had seen Bell visit the bank, earlier. Bell, Tinker decided, was in trouble. He had gone to the station after seeing Wheeler, and that meant that the banker had refused to loan him more money. There would be no other reason for him to ship cattle at this season. Sam Tinker had talked with Bell, he knew his plans, knew he wanted to build a herd instead of selling, knew that most of his stock was young.

Clay had ridden from town, and not long afterward Noble Wheeler had left the bank by the rear door, had mounted his gray horse and gone away into the desert. Tinker had been watching Wheeler long enough to know that the banker disliked riding. He never rode for pleasure. He particularly disliked riding in the desert at midday. Come to think of it, Tinker recalled, Wheeler never did anything for pleasure. Unless you called making money a pleasure.

One more item had been apparent to Tinker. Wheeler had carried a rifle when he rode out of town. That rifle had not been taken from the bank. It must, therefore, have been kept in the barn. And that barn was no place to leave a valuable rifle with so many strangers in town; and Noble Wheeler, who valued a dollar no more than his eyesight, was not likely to leave a rifle in such a place.

Suppose, then, it had only been taken to the barn on the previous night and hidden there?

And if so, why?

A few days later the grapevine brought added information to the grist of Sam Tinker's mill.

Clay Bell had been wounded when he charged the lumberjack camp in The Notch. Sam Tinker had listened to their excited talk, and all agreed that Bell had used his gun with his left hand. That his right side was bloody and he looked haggard.

Sam Tinker said nothing of these things, but sat quietly, listening, watching, and thinking.

Jim Narrows came walking up the street to dinner. Jim's

wife was gone to Denver and he was eating out these days.

"Howdy, Jim!" Tinker spat a stream of tobacco juice at an unoffending ant. "What's new?"

"Nothin' much." Narrows took his pipe from his mouth. He stood there, enjoying the coolness after the heat of the day. Then, low-voiced, he said, "Sam, what's got into Wheeler?"

"Wheeler? What's wrong?"

"He sent a wire down state tryin' to get that old killin' case against Monty Brown reopened." Narrows took his pipe from his mouth and stared into the bowl, then knocked it out against the edge of the porch. "A body would think Bell was havin' trouble enough without his own folks openin' up on him."

"Clay shippin' cows . . ."

"No cars—orders come down from main office. No cars for Bell."

"Devitt?"

"Prob'ly."

Sam Tinker turned the matter over in his mind. Bell owed Wheeler money. If Devitt logged off Bell's best range, Bell could never pay that money. It scarcely made sense that Wheeler would cut his own throat that way.

"Now I wonder?" he said aloud. Then added, "You know, Jim, we folks here in town, we should oughta stick together. This here Devitt—tryin' to ride roughshod over ever'body."

He rolled his quid in his jaws and spat again. It was too dark to see if he had nailed the ant again.

"Jim, you see any of the B-Bar outfit, you tell 'em to see me. That means Bell himself, too."

Jim Narrows put his pipe in his shirt pocket. "Never liked Noble Wheeler, anyway."

Sam Tinker did not follow Narrows into the dining room, although he customarily ate at this time. Instead, he sat in the darkness listening to the familiar evening sounds of the town. The lumberjacks were off the street now. They were a morose lot, not like the jacks he had known in his earlier days in Michigan, in the Saginaw country. Nor like

the old days in Tinkersville when sixteen thousand belted
men had been marching down to Hell the hard way.

It had been young and lusty then, with Indians in the
hills and every man packing a gun and a chip on his shoulder. That was when there had been a big strike back in the
hills and Cave Creek was alive. The old Tinker House had
worked three shifts a day, nine bartenders to the shift,
never closing its doors.

The Homestake had been big, too, and going all night.
The old Diamond Palace had burned down twelve years
ago, the night of the big wind when most of the town was
snuffed out like a candle.

His thoughts returned to the present. Noble Wheeler
had gone to the hills with a rifle, and he had never been
known to do any shooting before. Never even hunted deer
or sage hens. And he was not known to possess a rifle.
Showed you never really knew about a man.

One idea led to another, and this was Sam Tinker's night
for ideas. Somebody had told Devitt about that timber
on Deep Creek. It was not known to many away from the
town itself. It was not easily seen. Somebody knew it was
there, somebody who knew Devitt needed timber.

Sam Tinker heaved himself erect and walked into the
hotel. Beat all what a man could learn, "jest settin'." Folks
wasted a lot of time and tired a lot of horseflesh just gal-
livantin' around the country. Thing to do was "set to
home" and keep your eyes and ears open. Only ask questions when you had to. That was the ticket. Most folks
admired to talk. Just get them started and set by, they'd
tell you all they knew or suspected, soon or late.

Sam Tinker had no liking for Noble Wheeler. Nor for
Jud Devitt. More important, he had a warm affection for
Clay Bell.

Wheeler believed he knew a lot about Bell. In outward
facts, he knew a good bit. But he could have learned by
listening to Sam Tinker, who understood Clay, and who
knew on what shaky ground both Devitt and Wheeler
walked.

Had he not liked him before, he would have begun the
day he saw Devitt's lumberjacks, who had been swaggering

big around the town, come beefing it into town on their swollen and bloody feet.

The story had set the whole town to chuckling. Like Bell or not, and most people did, he was one of their own. Jim Narrows had passed the story down the wire until there were a lot of people laughing in Santa Fe and Las Vegas, and even Denver. Clay Bell had walked Jud Devitt's tough lumberjacks over twenty miles of desert in their sock feet. It was a story worth telling.

They heard it in Dodge, and there were some who were not surprised. "Know that boy," Bob Wright said. "They got off easy."

Sam Tinker sat in his nightly pinochle game with Jim Narrows, Ed Miller, and the postmaster. Pinochle helped him to think.

Jud Devitt was across the room, sitting over dinner with Judge Riley and his daughter. Jud had become aware during the day that he was losing prestige in Tinkersville. Not that it mattered, except to his ego. This was a small town in a backwater of the West—and he would show them. In his pocket was an appointment for a Deputy U. S. Marshal.

Yet despite the satisfaction of that appointment that rested in his pocket, to confer upon whom he liked, Devitt was not pleased. Judge Riley was not talkative tonight. He seemed preoccupied. And Colleen was, if not cool, at least no more talkative than her father.

Several times Devitt tried to warm up the conversation and guide it down pleasant channels, but without success. Colleen excused herself and retired to her room. Judge Riley crossed the room to watch Sam Tinker and his cronies at their pinochle game. Restless and irritable, Jud Devitt got to his feet and walked outside.

He had made his decision as to the marshal. It would be Morton Schwabe. The Dutchman disliked Bell, but Judge Riley, who would be asked to recommend the appointment, could not know that. The appointment of a local man who knew conditions was what Riley wanted.

The night was cool. He walked slowly down the street toward the corrals. If all panned out as he hoped, this situation would soon be right in the palm of his hand. But what else might Bell have up his sleeve? Irritably, Devitt looked at his dead cigar. The man had an uncanny way of planning ahead.

Colleen was not in bed. She had gone to her room, but she stood now beside the window looking out into the night.

She had changed. The few weeks that she had lived in Tinkersville had brought about a change in her feelings such as she had experienced in no previous period of her life. It was not only her feelings toward Jud, although they, too, had altered. It was something within herself. Her own world, the world of cities and parties and gaiety, seemed suddenly far away and very empty. Out here—she looked into the night and toward the lonely stars—it was different. She felt different, she was different.

Her friends had warned her against going west. She would be bored in a small town. There would be nothing to do. Jud would be busy. She had come on her own decision, overcoming Jud's objections and those of her father. And she was glad she had come.

The wind from the desert was soft. It brought intangible scents—sage, distant wood fire, the coolness of night. Somewhere a horse stamped and blew, and a tin-panny piano sounded from the saloon down the street, from the Homestake.

Down the street were empty buildings, and the foundations of those destroyed in the Fire. They always spoke of it so, for the Fire had been the biggest thing in their lives here, and it had been the final culmination of the mining boom. During her days in the town, while Jud and her father were busy, she had walked much and listened a lot. Dr. McClean was a man who enjoyed talking, and especially to a pretty woman. Sometimes when she helped him with Bert Garry she had listened to his talking of the old days. Once she had asked him about Bell.

"Clay?" The doctor paused, and seemed to be considering. "Colleen, he's a fine man. Sincere, hard-working. He drives himself harder than his men, but he's got a vein of poetry in him, too. And something else."

She waited, and when he did not speak again she adjusted the blanket over Garry, who was in a troubled sleep, aided by something the doctor had given him.

"Something else?"

"Yes . . . you remember the stories of the old Vikings? How they went berserk in battle? Clay's like that. He can be a cold, methodical, dangerous fighter up to a point, and then he goes completely hog-wild and reckless. Like the other night when he charged that campfire. The man would charge hell with a bucket of water."

"You like him, don't you?"

"Like him?" Dr. McClean paused briefly. "You bet I do."

CHAPTER 11

UNABLE TO sleep, Clay Bell was out of bed before the first light touched the tip of Piety. He got into his jeans and struggled into his boots. From where he sat on the edge of the bed he could look down the dark valley where the only light was the thin white streak of the trail to Tinkersville.

He sat very still, feeling the silence. He must get into town and see Garry.

Straightening to his feet, he walked outside and splashed cold water over the upper half of his body, then dipped his head in the bucket and dried himself with a rough towel. He was combing his hair when he heard a door slam and then the spash of water. Mahafee was up and busy.

Clay got into his shirt, and buckled on his gun belts. From the veranda he looked down valley, but there was as yet no light near the camp of Devitt's men. He crossed the hard-packed earth of the ranch yard, feeling the cold air coming down the pass. A rectangle of light showed at the kitchen window.

He gathered an armful of wood and carried it into the kitchen and dumped it into the box. Mahafee dried his hands on his apron and picked up the coffee pot. Without speaking, he filled a thick white mug with coffee and put it on the table. The kitchen smelled of woodsmoke, steam, and the fresh coffee. There was a comforting warmth from the woodstove.

Mahafee never talked at this hour and Bell respected the cook's feelings. Sitting down at the oilcloth-covered table, Bell tried to assay his position. Early morning, the kitchen sounds, and the warm fire seemed to help him think. He must have supplies, and if the fight were to continue he must have more hands, men who would fight. And who could fight.

The black coffee was scalding hot. He touched it to his

lips, then took it hastily away. Putting the cup down, he looked at his hands. He flexed the fingers on his right hand, feeling no pain. His shoulder was better, but far from well.

It was no use to think or plan now. So much depended on what Devitt did. Bell was irritated at leaving the initiative to him, but there was nothing else to do. And when he thought of Devitt his thoughts inevitably turned to Colleen.

It was impossible that she could love the man—yet why not? Love did strange things to people, and Devitt was a handsome man, if an obviously selfish one. Did she know he was entirely self-centered? Because he knew, that was no evidence that she perceived it.

Where would Judge Riley stand in the days to come? He had come to town with Devitt; apparently he was Devitt's man. Yet there was a strength to Riley's face that Bell detected beneath its seeming softness—a quiet man, not necessarily a pliable man.

He tried the coffee again. Still hot. Outside, footsteps crunched in the yard, and he heard the sound of the corral bars. That would be Hank Rooney. Hank always began his day by saddling a horse.

Hot cakes sputtered on the griddle and Bell could smell beef frying. Outside the window he could see a faint yellow above the rim of the far hills.

"Boss?"

Mahafee ran red work-coarsened hands over the floursack apron. "Boss, we'll be needin' grub. Short on flour an' coffee, mighty low on sugar. Need most everything else."

Clay flexed his hand again. Not reliable yet for a fast gun. He had always been ambidextrous, however, and his left hand was in good working order. But a trip to town for supplies was a vastly different thing from a trip to Doc McClean's. It meant loading a wagon in the street or behind the store. A perfect time for the lumberjacks' troublemaking efforts.

"Can we stall for a couple of days?"

"Might." Mahafee was dubious. "No longer."

Hank Rooney opened the door and came in. His face

looked fine-drawn in the morning light. He poured coffee, took a hasty swallow, then sat down on Bell's right.

"Who you figure fired that shot?"

Bell shrugged. "This morning I'll have a look around over there."

"You be careful." Rooney swallowed coffee and brushed his mustache with a finger.

Bill Coffin came in with Shorty Jones. Shorty had a heavy shock of hair, and he was brushing it now with his hand, and combing it back with his fingers. His shoulders bulged powerfully against the cloth of his shirt, and this morning his jaw looked hard.

Rooney looked suspiciously from Shorty to Coffin. The latter looked smug, as if he were about to put over something. Bill Coffin was a practical joker, and when he and Bert Garry had been riding as saddle partners there was always something popping. Shorty was more serious, a good hand with a gun, and nobody to push around. Since Garry had been hurt the two had been much together.

Coffin said something under his breath to Shorty. Jones hesitated, then said, "Maybe. We'll see."

On this morning when Clay stepped into the saddle he was riding a tough strawberry roan, a mountain horse, caught wild and broken to the saddle. The horse stepped out fast, wanting to go, and Clay put him up the trail through Emigrant Gap.

Long ago, before an easier route was found, this had been the way of the wagon trains in this part of the country. Just beyond the Gap there had been a massacre. Unsuspecting pioneers had been ambushed by Indians and almost wiped out. Only a few days before Devitt arrived in the country Clay had found an arrowhead there, and there were several old wagon wheels rolled out of the way against the rock wall.

He rode up the narrowing trail, emerging on the flatland inside the Gap. Here the country was open, with only a few scattered pines, thickening to clumps as one rode farther on.

Turning off the trail toward The Notch, Bell rode northwest into the timber, the roan's hoofs making almost no sound on the pine needles. Here, scattered among the pines, were the sycamores with their mottled trunks and a few oaks. On his left the mountain sloped steeply up, soon leaving behind the trees, emerging above their level in great bald shoulders of hard red rock and buff-colored cliffs streaked with long bands of white. The cliffs rose into serrated ridges and castled rocks, towering above the inner valley.

Here, in these few dozen square miles, surrounded by the outer desert and grassland, was a little oasis of green and verdant beauty. Away now from the ranch, walking the roan along the shoulder of the valley, Clay Bell found himself absorbing some of the quiet peace of the country. Below, on the edge of a far meadow, an antelope lifted his head, then bounded away. Suddenly a dozen others were running, disappearing into the trees.

Turning the roan downslope, he rode deeper into the forest, leaving the battlemented cliffs behind. On that side where lay the ranch in the mouth of Emigrant Gap, there was no trail into the inner basin except through the ranch. Ahead and still on his left, loomed the great bulk of Piety Mountain. A single trail led down Piety to the flat, that trail he had taken to intercept Colleen on her visit to the ranch. There was no other, and no man could approach or mount that trail without being visible to a watcher on the peak. Beyond Piety the wall of mountains swung westward, and there was but one trail down that side, the one Bell had used in his quick ride to Tinkersville, the one toward which he was now headed.

He watered the roan in Cave Creek, and then rode on. Skirting below wind-worn and rain-washed cliffs and leaving the ghost town far down the basin on his right, he took to the hills. He left the green shade and coolness behind as he rode up, moving from one shelf to the other, working his way higher and higher along the mountain. At the top there were clumps of cedar, and he drew up, glancing across the vast bottom toward the town.

A few trails of smoke lifted into the warm morning sunlight. It was nearly noon, and there was no movement along the road. He studied the terrain between the foot of the mountain and the town, but saw no sign of movement at all. With his glasses he studied the country longer and with infinite care.

Then he rode on. At this point it was nearly four thousand feet above the level country. Within the basin it was less than six hundred feet. Within there was coolness, grass, water, and the timber. Outside there was miles of bunchgrass country dotted with occasional clumps of mesquite, cat-claw, or cholla. When he came to the trail he rode to the bottom, then skirted it toward the spot from which the rifle shots had come.

He came upon the tracks suddenly. A small-hoofed horse had come up here. He studied the trail, working along until he found the place where the horse had stood, tied to a small clump of mesquite in a hollow, invisible from the trail.

The horse had stood here for some time. He studied the brush, hoping to find some indication of the color of the horse. But if the animal had scratched itself anywhere about, he was unable to find such a place.

The rider had been a heavy man with small feet. He trailed him along to the spot from where the shots had been fired. There were no cigarette butts, no exploded shells. Yet the presence of the man was plainly indicated. And he had been here for some time.

From the spot where he had waited there was an excellent view of the trail. Looking down from the low sandhill where the unknown marksman had waited, Clay Bell felt a little chill along his spine. His mouth felt dry and he backed up, wetting his lips. How the man had failed to kill him he could not guess. From here there was an excellent field of fire. He had been almost riding into the gun.

Tracks led to and from a boulder some distance off, and walking that way, he found a place which the unknown man had evidently considered as a place of ambush, but here two low trees obscured part of the trail. Yet the man had knelt there in the shadow, evidently sighting along his rifle. There in the sand, slightly damp near the boulder, was the plain print of a knee. The man had worn broadcloth trousers.

Automatically this eliminated all but a few men. Not many would be wearing such trousers across the range on a week-day. Later on, farther along the rider's homeward trail, he found where the man had drawn up to look back along his own path. There the horse had turned under the hand of the rider. Caught in the brush were a few tail hairs. The tail had been iron-gray.

Clay Bell returned to his own horse and mounted. Only when in the saddle did the significance of what he had discovered come home to him. Yet nothing in his suspicions seemed likely, for there was no motive.

Morton Schwabe was a huge, overbearing man who had been from boyhood a bully. Ranching in the country some miles from Deep Creek, he had no contact with Clay Bell except on his rare visits to town. Yet Morton Schwabe had taken a strong dislike to the quiet rancher who came and went about his business and seemed to be acquiring a respect in Tinkersville never given to himself.

There had been no trouble nor the occasion for it until Bell had stopped the big Dutchman from beating a horse. Angered, Schwabe had struck Bell. His next punch was a clean miss, but if Bell missed any at all they had been invisible punches, for Bell had promptly given him such a beating that it was three days before he could ride out of town. No man in a lifetime takes two such beatings. No man could take them.

When Jud Devitt approached Schwabe with the offer to be a Deputy U.S. Marshal he had accepted at once. For weeks he had been practicing with a pistol, a fact known only to Kesterson, who sold him ammunition, and now his chance had come and his mind was clearly made up. He would kill Clay Bell. And he would have the backing of the law.

Immensely pleased, he cleaned his gun and prepared to ride to town. He even brushed off his black coat, which he had not worn in months. He would go to town dressed as a marshal should be. He would take the papers and he would serve them.

Unaware of what had happened in Tinkersville, Clay

Bell rode back up the trail to the ridge. He studied the long sweep of land, and on the trail from the opposite direction to Tinkersville he saw a faint plume of dust. It was Jud Devitt returning from Schwabe's ranch, but Bell had no idea who the rider might be, nor what it signified.

He turned back into the now cooling depths of the woods, taking a new route back to the home ranch.

Wind murmured in the trees, bird calls came from the brush along the stream. Once he surprised a steer browsing in a quiet glade in the forest where sunlight slanted down through the columned trees. Coming out upon the rim of a plateau, he could look across the tops of the trees, across small meadows, along the winding courses of Cave Creek and Deep Creek to the far, striated shoulders of the mountains along The Notch.

Some of those firs were six or seven feet in diameter. There were sycamores down along Cave Creek that were equally thick. Those trees would never be cut off while he lived. This was his land, his home. ,

A branch of Cave Creek came chattering down the rocks and spilled through a long, narrow crevasse near him. He could hear it falling into a pool down in the darkness somewhere under the brush. He rode along, then drew up to look at a scuffed place down beside the stream. He could see the water from this one point, and the edge of the stream was scarred by boot prints.

Puzzled, he looked down at them. The narrow strip of sand was all of forty feet down and not easy to get at. He swung down and moved closer, then saw a place where a man might descend by stepping down upon the rocks and clinging to the branches of a sycamore. As he started down, he saw a scarred place on the bark made by a boot. Somebody else had preceded him, but not recently.

When he reached the bottom he saw a number of tracks, and under the overhang of the cliff was a sack that was bulky with its contents. Opening it, he found several chunks of what looked like ore. They were heavy and metallic.

The tracks had been made within the past month—no,

within the past three weeks. There had been a rain before that that would have washed them out.

Somebody had been here, working. Somebody who wanted that ore, and somebody who did not want his presence known.

Somebody who might be willing to kill to get what he wanted.

CHAPTER 12

JUD DEVITT was immensely pleased. Morton Schwabe had accepted the appointment as Deputy Marshal and would serve the papers on Clay Bell, forcing him to open a right-of-way through Emigrant Gap and The Notch. It would be none too soon, for valuable time had been lost and already there had been requests from officials of Mexican Central for information as to when the first load of ties would be received.

He found Judge Riley at dinner with Colleen. Both looked up as he approached. For an instant it seemed there was a coolness in their manner, but this he promptly dismissed as unreasonable. He seated himself. Colleen, he realized suddenly, was even more attractive than he had believed. She was a lovely girl . . . a lovely woman.

He had been neglecting her, but business was business and this affair had given him more trouble than he expected. But now, he assured them, the trouble was all over and when the papers were served there would be nothing to keep them from logging off Deep Creek. In a short time they could move on, back to New York if they wished.

"I seem to remember you were quite sure when we came here that you'd have no trouble," Colleen suggested, a tinge of irony in her tone. "You're very confident."

He waved a dismissing hand. "My boys are ready to move. Schwabe will serve the papers tomorrow."

"Schwabe?" It was the first time Colleen had heard a mention of just who had received the appointment. "Isn't that asking for trouble?"

Her father put down his cup. "Why do you say that?"

Devitt started to interrupt but Colleen persisted. "There's been trouble between Schwabe and Clay. Doctor McClean told me about it."

Riley's face was stern. "You said nothing of this, Jud."

Devitt shrugged. He was irritated by Colleen's inter-
ference in what was man's business. She knew nothing of
such things.

"A detail, Judge. Competent men aren't to be found
everywhere."

"Or men who will take orders."

Jud Devitt's face flushed, but he turned on Colleen,
smiling. "If one wishes to get something done he has to
use the tools at hand. Now let's forget business. Let's talk
about us."

"Us?"

Jud Devitt had never been a tactful man. Impatient to
get on with things, he usually put down any idea that Colleen expressed as a mere whim. He was sure she was dis-
pleased because of his neglect.

"Colleen," he put his hand over hers, "we've delayed too
long now. Why don't we get married right away?"

"Jud," her voice was quiet, and she looked straight into
his eyes, "I'm not going to marry you. Not now or at any
time."

Jud Devitt was shocked. He started to speak, then
stopped. His face, which had paled, suddenly flushed.

"What sort of a joke is this?"

"You're a handsome man, Jud, and a strong man. You
have done big things, and I admired you for it. But I never
understood until now how you did them."

Anger stirred him. Judge Riley sat very quiet, and continued to eat. Devitt looked from the judge to his daughter, trying to stifle his anger and to control his voice.

"You know, Jud," she continued, "some big things are
done by men who are really very small."

"Just what do you mean by that?"

"Given time," she responded coolly, "I think you'll find
out for yourself, but today I learned that the attack on
those poor boys was made by your direct order."

"And so?" He was really angry now. His dark eyes narrowed and his face held its flush.

"If Bert Garry dies you'll be his killer."

"Don't be a fool!" His anger flared. The idea that this

girl should call him to account enraged him. "Bell attacked Williams! They began it."

"Not according to Wat."

Devitt pushed back his chair. "Judge," he kept his voice even, "you'd better take this daughter of yours and talk some sense into her." He got up, then looked down at Colleen. "We'll be married this week or not at all."

"Not at all," she said, and she watched him, startled at the cruel lights in his eyes. This was a man she had never known. "And if you make any more trouble for Clay Bell I'll hate you as long as I live."

"So that's it? You've fallen in love with that cowhand!" He turned abruptly, knocking over his chair, and strode from the room.

Only Sam Tinker sat near enough to have distinguished their words. Despite her anger, she had to smile, for Sam was making no effort to conceal his pleasure. He was fairly beaming, and when he smiled his face became so much the picture of good humor that one could only smile in return.

She sat very still, looking down at her plate. She was no longer hungry. Jud was gone—and her only feeling was of relief She looked up suddenly. "Dad, did I do right?"

"I think so. I think we've both been saved from a serious mistake."

Jud Devitt had walked outside into the night. He took a cigar from his pocket and bit off the end. He was furious, seething inside.

He lighted his cigar and stared down the street. Let up on Clay Bell? He'd be eternally damned if he did! Then he remembered the curious expression on Morton Schwabe's face when he accepted the appointment. Bell was not out of trouble by a long shot.

Across the street a man loitered, and Devitt glanced sharply at him. It was Stag Harvey. As he looked, the man sauntered off down the street, and Devitt's eyes followed him.

Suddenly a horseman rounded into the street and came down the avenue at a dead run. Seeing Devitt, he drew up sharply. "Boss! We're burned out! The whole camp!"

"What's that?"

The man stammered in his excitement, then calmed down. "Right after dark, Jud. Some feller out on the desert called out, called for help. Called some of the boys by name!"

Jud Devitt's fury was gone Now he felt something cold and murderous within him—a feeling he had never known before.

"We rushed out, figurin' some of the boys was in trouble. We couldn't find a thing, but then we saw the whole camp was in flames. We rushed back an' fought fire most of an hour. Lost two wagons, burned right down to the wheel rims, all the grub, and the donkey engine mighty near ruined."

"Who did you see? Which of those cowhands did it?"

"Never saw anybody, Boss! We had to fight fire an' whoever done it, if anybody did, they got away."

Devitt remained where he was when the messenger had gone with his orders. Tomorrow the whole town would be laughing at him. And Colleen behaving like a silly school girl!

His cigar tasted terrible. He took it from his mouth and threw it into the street.

There was a donkey engine in Holbrook. He could send for that if his own could not be repaired immediately. But probably it was only the platform—he would have a look at it first thing in the morning.

And tomorrow Morton Schwabe would serve his papers. Jud Devitt decided he could wait. That would be triumph enough, to send his wagons through the Gap. He could wait—although every time he thought of Bell he wished he could live over that day in the street when he walked away from Bell's cool challenge.

His anger cooled into resolution. He would show them. He would show them all what it meant to buck Jud Devitt.

From his seat on the porch Sam Tinker watched Jud walk away down the street. He had seen the rider come, had overheard his excited words. Sam needed no questions—in the burning of the wagons and the manner in which it was consummated he could see the ripe, rich hand of Bill Coffin. He chuckled fatly and rubbed his jaw. It was just as much fun as being young again, to sit here and enjoy it, without all the riding and sweating.

He looked across at the bank, dark and silent now. Nor was there a light upstairs. Noble Wheeler was a restless man these days.

He liked sitting here, smelling the cool evening wind from off the sage levels, and once in a while a faint scent of the pines atop Piety. He could sit here on his porch and smell all the smells. Old Mrs. Weber was working late over her washing. Jim Narrows was cooking over a cedar fire again. And occasionally he imagined he got a whiff of the smoke from off the burned wagons at the Gap, miles away. Too far, actually, but he could imagine it.

There was a new tenant in a cottage in the block beyond Doc McClean's. She had come to town a few days after the lumberjacks, and for some days Sam had believed that explained her arrival, yet she had no visitors. Not at first.

She was blond and lovely, a somewhat overstuffed blonde with a friendly, agreeable face. Her figure was one that turned heads when she walked by. This was the blonde Bill Coffin had seen, the blonde who was keeping him awake too many nights, just thinking about her.

Yet she was not without visitors—or a visitor. Jud Devitt had been to call, but evidently all had not gone well, for he had not stayed long. Sam Tinker did not know that Bill Coffin had seen the blonde—what was more important, the blonde had seen him. He had those lean, rawboned good looks and that whimsical humor that can be vastly appealing.

Sam Tinker was enjoying the smells of the night and his memories of the blonde when he heard the soft footfalls of a walking horse. He heard the horse stop in the darkness alongside the hotel. He heard the creak of saddle leather as a man swung down.

Sam Tinker could wait. Whatever he had that anyone might want would be locked in the safe inside, and folks in the Deep Creek country knew better than to rob Sam Tinker. Sam had too many friends. Sheriffs and outlaws, ranchers and sheepmen, Indians from off the high mesas and prospectors from the rough country beyond The Notch. So he waited, puffing contentedly on his pipe. Whatever happened, it would make his evening more interesting.

The steps creaked and he looked up to see Clay Bell standing beside him. Clay hunkered down on his heels at the side of the chair. A man would have to walk clear past to even see him, squatting like that.

"Howdy, Clay! Cuttin' a wide swath, these days."

"Know a man who owns a gray horse with small hoofs?" Clay, without changing position, began to build a smoke. "High-steppin', nervous sort of horse. This man would be wearin' store-bought pants."

Sam Tinker inhaled and held it, then let the smoke drift from his lips. He was vastly pleased by the question. He was a disciple of the belief that evil always gets what it deserves, and he enjoyed seeing his philosophy borne out. Particularly in this case. He had a certain admiration for really hard men who were skilled killers if they walked up to a man's face and gave him a chance, but not for the gunman who lay in ambush, and who shot in the back.

"Mighty small field, Clay. Tibbott, he's out o' town somewheres. Doc McClean's busy with that cowhand o' yours. Kesterson ain't been off the sidewalk for two months."

"Jud Devitt?"

"Couldn't say. Mostly he rides a buckboard or that bay hoss he got from Feeney. Hear he had him a run-in with that filly of Judge Riley's. She took up for you."

Ordinarily, this would have distracted Clay. Tonight it did not. Later he would remember it, but for now there was another problem.

Suppose he eliminated Jud Devitt? And shooting from cover did not seem like Devitt's way. Morton Schwabe? He had never seen the man in a store-bought suit—not the pants, anyway.

Noble Wheeler.

It made no sense. Wheeler had been instrumental, he now believed, in getting Devitt to come to Tinkersville; he might have done other things, but the small profit in a timber venture was hardly enough—at least, the small part that Wheeler would get.

The man who had waited for him knew of the path up the mountain. Whoever it was that had climbed down the bank and knocked those samples off the wall had used that path. A party of men could not approach it unseen. Nothing but a man afoot or a rider would climb it, and a rider on a good mountain horse.

If that ore now, if that ore was valuable . . . If it was gold—but it was not. Clay Bell knew gold when he saw it.

"Wheeler have a gray horse?"

Sam Tinker spat into the darkness off the end of the porch. "Keeps a couple of horses in the stable back of the bank. Wouldn't take a man long to find out!"

Clay Bell dropped his cigarette and rubbed it out with his toe. Then he stepped off the porch into the darkness. Waiting until there was no one visible along the street, he walked slowly across. Had anyone come out Bell would have appeared to be only another puncher going casually about his lack of business.

This town was alive with danger for him. His life would not be worth a plugged peso if either Devitt or Wheeler— if Wheeler was his man—knew he was in town. Devitt might not have him killed, he would certainly like to see him maimed.

All was dark behind the bank. Bell walked along, hesitated, looking up at the dark windows. Was there a face there? Imagination . . .

The stable door was open, and there were three horses. The one in the end stall was a gray. His lighted match told him that. The horses rolled their eyes at him, and the gray blew nervously. Bell lowered the match . . . the hoofs were small, well-shaped, freshly shod. The tracks were plain to see in the earth of the stable floor—and they were familiar.

Clay Bell straightened and blew out his match. For an instant he held it, smelling the sulphur and thinking. Then he walked outside. Only when he was away from the stable did he drop the match.

CHAPTER 13

BILL COFFIN had a memory for a pretty face. And his raid on the Devitt road camp had whetted his appetite for more such attacks. In either case, a waiting game was no part of his way of life.

Shorty was in a receptive mood. He had been anxious to see Bert Garry, and now that the tide of battle had turned their way, it looked like a chance to slip away to town. Rooney was at the ranch, and as far as he knew, Clay was also. And there was always Mahafee, never to be ignored when battle was in prospect.

Moreover, his mind had been unable to let go the feeling of horror remaining from the night he had seen Pious Pete Simmons boot Garry into unconsciousness. No stranger to the rougher sides of life, Shorty Jones had grown up in a land and a time when men fought with guns, with knives, and more rarely with their fists. But to jump in the face of a man already down with calked boots was the ultimate in ugliness.

"All right," he agreed finally, "let's go."

Bill Coffin was as concerned with the blonde as with carrying the war to the enemy camp. If she was a dance hall girl she would be at the Homestake. Saddling up, they moved out cautiously so as to alarm neither Hank Rooney nor the men at the road camp. Neither man was unaware of the danger that lay ahead. Tinkersville was teeming with lumberjacks, and those who had been forced to walk to town in their sock feet were eager for some chance to retaliate.

Unaware that Coffin and Jones had started toward town, Clay Bell left the stable and, after a glance up at the dark windows of Wheeler's quarters, he walked back to the street.

At the Tinker House and the Homestake, lights were bright and there was the sound of tin-panny music and loud laughter. Occasionally a man appeared on the street, walking toward the bunkhouse or to another saloon. As he waited in the shadows, Colleen Riley came from the hotel and, after pausing for a word with Sam Tinker, came down the steps and turned up the street toward Doc McClean's.

Standing in the deep shadow, his hat pulled low, he watched her pass the window, saw the momentary light upon her face, and heard the rustle of her skirts. Back in the stable a horse stamped, and somewhere a door slammed.

Clay Bell glanced sharply down the street, his eyes going from door to door with quick, searching glance, and then he stepped out of the darkness and crossed the street toward Colleen.

She turned quickly as she heard his steps, and he spoke. "Oh! It's you," she said.

He fell into step beside her. Back on the porch, Sam Tinker rolled his pipe in his lips and spat. Things were looking up.

"You shouldn't be in town, you know."

He liked the sound of her voice, and the suggestion of worry that was in it.

"I wanted to see Bert." When they had taken a few steps he added, "And to thank you for all you've done for him. Doc's a great fellow, but no comfort to a man when he's down."

"I've been glad to do what I could." She stopped and put her hand on his arm. Her face was shadowed with worry. "Clay, Bert has pneumonia. We've been afraid of that."

Clay Bell stared down the street. If Bert had pneumonia he might die. And if Bert Garry died, Clay knew there would be no holding the B-Bar. His boys would come to town, with or without him, and they would leave dead men on the street. Not even he could stop or prevent it, for these men rode for the brand and possessed a fierce, almost feudal loyalty for those with whom they rode. And Bert Garry had been the youngest of the lot, and a favorite.

"There'll be trouble if he doesn't pull through. Two years ago rustlers killed a rider of mine. We trailed them down. Bert and I, we circled around a hill to cut off anybody who escaped. Before we could get up the boys had killed all four rustlers and set fire to the place."

"I've tried to tell Jud. So have others."

Where they stood there was deep shadow. Out over the desert a coyote spoke to the moon, his shrill voice yapping sounds that trailed away and died. He stood silent, wanting to speak of other things, yet uncertain of how to begin.

"He's different these days," she said finally. "Not like himself."

"Jud's a front runner, Colleen. He's used power and money to win, and he is used to winning. I think he has always had an advantage before."

"I'm afraid of what he may do if he begins to think he'll lose."

"He will lose."

They were silent again, and almost automatically they began to walk on toward McClean's together.

"And then what will you do?" he asked suddenly. "If he loses, I mean?"

"I don't know. Father may go back East. But he likes it here, and this was a temporary appointment." She looked around at him. "Jud engineered it. I suppose you know?"

"I figured so."

"Clay—did you know about Morton Schwabe?"

"What about him?"

She explained quickly, and saw his face stiffen with surprise, then grow grave. "The man's a brute. Not fit for any commission. And he's an enemy of mine."

She told him about the injunction and Devitt's plan— that Schwabe was to serve it. He held himself still, considering all it might mean. Here again was evidence of a guiding hand that must be that of Noble Wheeler. By himself, it was doubtful if Devitt would have arrived at the choice of Schwabe for marshal. That had to be suggested to him by someone who knew of the rancher's enmity for Bell.

Also, it gave an indication of the lengths to which Devitt was prepared to go. Schwabe was a troublemaker, and with the authority of the law behind him he could be a dangerous man. Kesterson had several times informed Bell of Schwabe's continued purchase of ammunition, that could only mean constant practice with a gun.

Devitt might yet come to the hiring of killers. It had not yet been done, but without doubt this latest choice meant that, although he had not hired a killer, he was not above trying to arrange a killing. Such papers could have been served peaceably by a dozen men, but never by Schwabe. It was a deliberate effort either to have Bell killed or to put him in the position of resisting the Federal law.

"If that injunction is served," he said slowly, "I'll have to honor it. I won't buck the government." An idea came to him suddenly. "There's a way of beating this yet."

He hesitated, thinking. "If Devitt is allowed to use that road, he'll start cutting timber as soon as he's on the land. Colleen, how strong is Devitt with your father?"

"He's lost ground, Clay. Dad did think Jud could do no wrong until he heard that Devitt had ordered Duval and Simmons to attack Garry."

"What?" Clay caught her arm. "Devitt ordered that attack?"

She looked up, frightened by his expression. "Didn't you know? He wanted to make you short-handed. Bob Tripp didn't like it too well, but he passed on the order. They were overheard, and Jud admitted it to me."

Clay Bell dropped his grip from her arm. "Colleen, if Bert Garry dies I'll kill Jud Devitt."

"No—no, Clay! That will only make matters worse."

They had reached the door of the McClean home. A light burned in the office; another, a dim light, in Garry's room.

A thought came to Clay. It was an idea that had come to him a few minutes before, but had been lost when he heard that Devitt had ordered the attack on Garry. He turned the idea over in his mind now.

"Is your father at the hotel?"

"Yes, but be careful. The saloon is filled with lumber-jacks."

He watched her go into the house, then turned abruptly and went back down the street. As he walked, his eyes and ears alert for trouble, he thought of what he planned. It looked good, it looked very good.

Judge Riley sat over coffee and cigars with Sam Tinker in the hotel dining room. Clay stepped into the door and looked quickly around. There was no one else in sight. Loud voices came from the saloon beyond the swinging doors that divided it from the lobby. Clay crossed the lobby, entered the dining room and joined the two men at the table.

"Judge, you've issued an injunction that will allow Devitt to use the old stage road, is that right? Until this case is settled?"

Riley nodded, waiting.

"All right, that's fair enough. Now I want an injunction forbidding any cutting of timber until the case is settled. This injunction should also deny any camping along the road."

"You believe he would begin cutting before the government has made a ruling?"

"Don't you?"

Tinker hitched himself around in his chair and spoke. "He could have his timber cut before any ruling was passed down. Fact is, he has a man, name of Chase, acting for him in Washington. He could block any settlement of the case, then he could pay a modest sum in damages if the ruling went against him."

"And I'd have lost my grazing when I need it most."

Riley tasted his coffee. It was too hot. He put the cup down carefully and considered the question. Knowing Jud Devitt, he realized the man had no intentions of waiting for any final decision. He could not afford to wait. Yet if he gave Bell the injunction he wanted, Devitt would be furious. He would do all he could to break the judge. And he was an old man with a daughter to consider.

Then he smiled thoughtfully. It was too easy to judge a case by self-interest. Too easy, and wrong. What Clay

Bell asked was reasonable and right. It would prevent Devitt from cutting timber he had no right to cut, anyway.

It was Sam Tinker who decided him. "Might prevent bloodshed," Sam said, stoking his pipe. "Schwabe would attempt to enforce that injunction for Devitt. This new move would stop them cold. Schwabe would kill Clay if he could do it under cover of the law—but he would not go against the law itself. I'll gamble on it."

Judge Riley tried his coffee again. It was black, hot, and strong. He drank, then put down his cup. "I'll grant your injunction. I'll issue it tonight."

"Good!" Clay came to his feet. Then he hesitated for a moment. "Judge, when this is over, I'd like your permission to speak to your daughter."

Judge Riley looked up sharply. He measured the man before him, the strong, clean-cut features, the bronzed face and the quiet eyes. Yes—yes, of course.

He nodded, "Young man, you've my permission, for what it's worth. Colleen has been taught to make her own decisions."

"Thank you, sir."

Clay Bell turned and went out. Riley stared after him. "These young people! I— Sam, you make your coffee too blasted hot!"

Stag Harvey was loafing on the steps when Bell came out. Clay paused, studying him.

"Still around, Stag?"

The man's slow smile was non-committal. "Yeah, still here."

"You might as well drift. This trouble's over."

"Don't make any bets."

Jack Kilburn came out of the saloon. "Stag—we got business."

Harvey turned away. "'By, Clay. Be seein' you!"

Bell watched them go, then turned toward his horse. All he wanted now was to get out of town. Riley would issue his injunction, and Schwabe, bully though he was, would be up against a stacked deck. They would allow free passage, and to avoid trouble, he, Clay Bell, would remain carefully out of sight. Then Schwabe would have to protect the trees himself. He wouldn't like it, but he would do it. Schwabe might be many things, but he had a wholesome respect for the law.

Boot heels sounded on the walk, and Bell drew back into a doorway. A fast-walking man was coming toward him. And the man was angry. He could tell by the sound of those heels.

He stood very still and watched the man pass. It was Jud Devitt. Had he reached out a hand he could have touched him.

Unknown to Bell, Jud Devitt had just had the final blow administered to his ego. He had been told, not too gently, where he could go. Told by a blonde named Randy Ashton, a blonde whom Devitt had invited to Tinkersville and who he believed would prove sufficiently pliable and willing. Faced with an abrupt ultimatum she had proved anything but easy, and had, with considerable dignity, ordered him to leave. As he turned away a rider had dismounted at the door.

Angry words flooded to Devitt's lips and he turned abruptly, jerking open the door. Before he could get out a word, a soft voice, yet one edged with a chill quality he did not mistake, said, "You was just leavin', wasn't you?"

The tall young man was a blond cowhand, the one who had grinned so impudently the day in the street when Bell laid down his quiet challenge. Beside himself with fury, Devitt was about to speak, and then he saw there was no impudence in the cowpuncher's eyes, and that the man's hand rested on the butt of his gun.

Without a word, Devitt turned and went down the steps. He did not glance back, but he knew the man was waiting there, making sure that he left. Filled with fury and humiliation, Jud Devitt was in no condition to notice anyone. He walked past Clay Bell and headed for the Tinker House.

Almost at the hotel a man stepped from the shadows. He stepped directly into Devitt's path.

"Mr. Devitt? Maybe we could talk business now."

Clay Bell saw the man, and he heard the words. But

he did not recognize the man, who stood in partial darkness, nor did he recognize the voice.

Devitt's voice came, after momentary hesitation. "Yes,
come along."

Bell walked to his horse and stepped into the leather.
It was time he returned to the ranch, but he sat there, the
thoughts churning in his head. He had measured the
anger and fury in Devitt just now, and he knew the man
in this frame of mind was capable of any sort of violence.
He couldn't stop Devitt from getting on his land, for
the injunction had already been processed. But his move
to stop Devitt from logging until the courts decided the
issue was an effective legal counteraction. The only thing,
Clay knew, was that when Devitt found out about it,
anything might happen.

It struck him that it would be better to be right here on
the spot when Devitt found out about it. Maybe the whole
thing could be settled one way or another, right then. The
thought of spending the night in the hotel didn't appeal to
him, but Hank was out at the ranch, and that was good
enough for Clay.

He turned his horse and headed for the livery, feeling a
lift of spirit. His mood would have been less agreeable if he
had recognized the man who had stopped Devitt.

It was Jack Kilburn.

CHAPTER 14

THE EVENTS leading up to that night had been not unusual, and there was about them nothing not to have been expected in the normal course of human relations. Their importance was due to the time of their happening, only indirectly to the events themselves. They were, in many respects, a culmination. Of all those concerned, the one most aware of what was happening was the man only indirectly concerned, Sam Tinker.

Jud Devitt was a man with an eye for a well upholstered blonde, and he had seen Randy Ashton singing in a dance hall. Randy, he had been advised, was hard to get. Jud had permitted himself a smile, and nothing that happened immediately thereafter had caused him reason to doubt the thought behind the smile. He was not the first man to misunderstand the workings of the feminine mind. He had his motives. Randy Ashton had hers.

Jud Devitt was a handsome man with plenty of money. Randy was entertaining in Julesberg. They had talked one evening and Randy had been tempting but evasive. Randy was a girl who knew what she had and knew where it was wanted, yet underneath the glittering appearance and the apparently compliant manner was a girl who had grown up on a cow ranch. The daughter of a rancher and the sister of cowhands, a girl who could cook a meal as good as any man might wish to eat, a girl who could, when necessary, handle a six-horse team or rope a steer, and who had, at twelve, loaded guns for her father and brothers during an Indian attack on their homestead.

Unsuccessful on that attempt, the Indians had caught her father halfway to town and left him without his hair. Her brother Ben had been going over the trail to Wyoming when the herd took off in a stampede, and his friends buried what was left of him on the banks of the Platte. Pete, a husky lad and the sole support of his sister, lost a running argument with Apaches and left Randy with no relatives, no money, and no prospects.

One thing she knew how to do. She could sing. All her family had been singers and she had grown up singing the Scotch and Irish folk songs that were the heritage of her people. The songs of the East came west with its people and she had learned those, and so when Pete was killed, Randy began singing. Later she learned to dance. She had always known how to handle men.

Julesberg's boom slowed to a walk, and Jud, not yet aware that his fiancée was to accompany her father to Tinkersville, had written her suggesting she come on and join him. The letter had been sufficiently ambiguous to imply a lot of things, and his intentions seemed serious.

Not long after her arrival she discovered his intentions were serious enough, but not exactly what she had expected. She had to admit they had not been entirely unsuspected, either.

Yet a climax had been postponed, due to the sudden turn of events for Jud Devitt. Colleen had arrived with her father and the Deep Creek timber had not fallen easily into his hands.

In the meantime, Randy had seen Bill Coffin, just as he had seen her.

Randy made discreet inquiries of Kesterson as to who Bill Coffin was, and Kesterson, dryly but not without understanding, had told her. And the storekeeper, of whom no one suspected a sense of humor, was fully aware of Bill's weakness for jokes, and appreciated them. So the report on Bill Coffin had not been lacking in color.

Later, when Bill met Randy, he proceeded to give even more glowing and picturesque accounts of himself, and, coupled with wavy hair and an engaging grin, they had their effect.

Randy Ashton was a girl who looked as if born to a dance hall, but she was a girl whose heart only beat in tune to cotton print and kitchens. She had grown up with cowhands, and Bill Coffin was a cowhand.

Jilted by his fiancée, at least temporarily, Jud Devitt remembered the blonde. He beat a path to her door and

was received politely, but his suggestions fell upon ears
apparently deaf. A more direct suggestion met with a quiet
refusal and the pointed implication that he would find the
air agreeable.

This unexpected stubbornness where he had expected
compliance had been the final straw. He burst out into
the night only to see Bill Coffin dismounting. Their brief
encounter had sent him away a poor second, and he could
imagine them laughing at him. As a matter of fact, neither
had given him another thought.

It was late when Bill Coffin left Randy. He stepped
into the saddle and rode slowly down the street. Shorty
was around town. They had best get together and start
back for the ranch.

Drawing up before the Homestake, Coffin leaned forward and peered into the window. There was no sign of
Shorty. The place was crowded with lumberjacks. Nor
was there a B-Bar horse tied at Doc McClean's.

Coffin swung down and checked with the doctor. Garry
was restless and had a bad fever. It was better not to dis-
turb him. Shorty Jones had come and gone hours ago. So
had Clay.

Stepping back into the saddle, Bill Coffin soft-footed
his horse down the street, keeping to the shadows. Clay
Bell was in town, and that meant that Rooney was alone
at Emigrant Gap! Unless Shorty had started back, and
Bill doubted that Shorty would go back without him.

A lumberjack came from the stable leading several
teams. He walked with them to the watering trough. Bill
Coffin, suddenly alert, waited in the shadows. More lumberjacks came from the stable, all carrying rifles. Other
men were already gathering around three wagons.

Bill turned his horse. No time to look for Shorty now.
He walked his horse down an alleyway, eased around the
livery stable corral, and rode between two haystacks and
into the cottonwoods along the creek. The night was cool
and there was a faint smell of woodsmoke. He reached the
desert and started his horse on a lope for the Gap. Then,
changing his mind suddenly, he turned his horse and
started across the desert toward Piety Mountain. The cool

wind fanned his cheeks and he rode swiftly, holding his horse to a steady pace, weaving among clumps of grease-wood and racing by the looming shadows of mesquite. The trail up Piety was heavy going.

Stacked high on Piety was the dry wood of the signal fire that would bring in the guards and the men riding with the cattle. With Rooney, Rush Jackson, and Montana Brown— He chuckled. They could come! They could come and stand ten deep all across the Pass!

A half-hour later, even as the rumbling wagons rolled out of town, he was dropping to his knees beside the stack of wood. He brushed dried leaves together, a bit more dry grass, then placed a lighted match. Flame caught and curled, smoke lifted, then the tongues of the flame lapped at the dry branches, twisting hungrily about the cedar and the pine. They leaped, caught, crackled. . . .

The late stage rumbled to a stop at the stage station and Stag Harvey, loafing on the street with two belted guns, watched a big, loose-jointed man in a rumpled suit get down from the stage carrying a worn leather traveling bag.

"How are you, Stag? Clay around?"

"Down to the hotel, I think."

"You might as well light a shuck, Stag. The war's over. At least, it will be when I talk to Judge Riley."

"Maybe." Stag smiled past his cigarette. "That'll be no good news for Jack an' me. We need money."

Tibbott started on, then caught by a sudden thought, he stopped abruptly. "Stag, never knew you to wear two guns unless you were working."

Stag Harvey straightened from the post. "You can tell Clay that, Tibbott. Tell him I'm workin'. Both Jack an' me."

"Don't do it, Stag."

"You tell him."

"Stag, he don't wear that gun for show. He's no pil-grim."

"Didn't figure so."

Hardy Tibbott walked on, more swiftly now. It was good

to be back, but he did not like to think of that man
standing back there by the stage station. With either Kilburn or Harvey, Bell might have a chance, but with both?

Ed Miller looked up as the tired man dropped his bag.
"Hey! Bell's been askin' for you, almost every day. He was
beginning to believe you were dead."

"Dead tired, is all."

He looked around at Sam Tinker. "Stag Harvey's wearing both guns."

"The hell you say!"

"Saw some wagons leaving for the Gap, too."

Sam Tinker turned on his chair. "Ed, you get up those
stairs and tell Clayl Quick now!"

The door shoved open and Shorty Jones came in. His
barrel chest spread the wool shirt taut over its muscles.
He looked quickly around the room, then at Tibbott.
"The boss will be glad to see you."

"Who's at the ranch, Shorty?"

"Rooney. Coffin came in with me."

"Coffin's gone back." The speaker was a tall, lazy-
looking man. "Shuttin' my hen house when I saw him
ease down the alley and then go hell a-whoopin' into the
desert."

Stag Harvey pushed open the door and came in, glancing
around as if to check those present. His eyes went to
Jones. There was no love lost between the two, but Stag
jerked his head toward the Gap.

"Looks like a fire on Piety. Can't see the fire, but there's
a reflection."

"That's Coffin." Shorty tucked his thumbs behind his
belt. He had not missed the fact that Harvey wore both
guns. "He's with Rooney by now."

"You spoke too soon, Tibbott," Harvey said, "the fight's
just started."

Shorty Jones turned to face him. He was cocked for
trouble and Stag Harvey could see it. "Believe me, Stag,
it's over. You and Kilburn better rattle your hocks."

Harvey smiled. This man was tough and dangerous,
but Harvey was not interested in fighting for fun. He used

his gun for pay; it was a cold, simple business. "Maybe, Shorty. Maybe we will."

He opened the door to step out, and Colleen came in. Her face was pale, her eyes dark with foreboding. "Bert!" she spoke quickly. "Where's Clay? Bert's dead!"

"Dead?" Several voices echoed the word, one of them Harvey's.

The bat-wing doors to the saloon fanned sharply and they looked around. "Who was that? Who went out?"

"It was Shorty Jones." Ed Miller's voice was low, unintentionally dramatic. "Better look to your hole-card, Stag."

"Shorty? And Bert Garry dead? Then God help Pete Simmons!"

Stag Harvey stood on the street rolling a smoke. He was sweating, although the night was cool. Better than anyone, he could appreciate what the death of Bert Garry would mean to a tough outfit like the B-Bar. Ed's advice had been good. It was time to look to their hole-card. But where was Jack?

He lighted up, inhaled, and quickly ran over in his mind the places Jack might be. They had not been sure that Clay was in town—but he was.

Had it not been for the presence of Shorty, Stag might have gone upstairs after Clay and played a lone hand. But Shorty was tough enough by himself, and Sam Tinker would not sit idle, nor would Hardy Tibbotts. Innkeeper and lawyer, but both had used guns in their time.

If the B-Bar was going on the warpath they had best get their job done and split the breeze getting out of town.

Clay Bell had waited no longer than it took to pull on his boots and belt his guns. He wanted to see Tibbott, but there was no time for talk with an attack beginning at the ranch. He went down the back steps, crossed to the corral and saddled up.

The fire was still burning when he started for Piety. There was dust lingering in the air, dust from the passage of wagons.

It was not until he was nearly at the beginning of the

climb up Piety Mountain that he recalled he had asked
Tibbott nothing about Washington! Too late now—that
could wait. He took the trail up the mountain, and when
at last he topped the rise there was only the lingering of
woodsmoke in the air, and the few embers of the signal
fire.

He started down the short trail to the ranch, and had
scarcely taken it before he heard, faint and far away, the
sound of a rifle shot.

CHAPTER 15

HANK ROONEY was no fool. Shortly after Shorty and Bill slipped away, he became aware of the unusual silence around the place. A casual round of the buildings and a check of saddles showed him the two riders were gone. It took no great amount of imagination to guess their destination.

There was, he knew, no immediate danger of an attack, yet if Devitt realized that he was alone he might attempt to force a way through.

He was too seasoned a campaigner to leave anything to doubt. Preparations for an attack had been made long before this, but he made the rounds and checked all the available weapons. Bert Garry's Winchester was in the bunkhouse. Hank brought it to the house and loaded it.

He had two Sharps .50 buffalo guns, a Spencer .56, and an express shotgun.

Again he studied the Gap. All was empty and still. He threw more hay to the horses. Suddenly the ranch began to feel very lonely. Night came quickly in the narrow space between the cliffs and the darkness crept down and engulfed the ranch while the far-off hills were still touched with light.

Long since, every man on the ranch had learned the range to the opening of the Gap. By day there was no cover in the last two hundred yards. By night it was another story.

Somewhere a coyote yapped the moon. A wind stirred the cottonwood leaves, and Hank Rooney walked up on the porch of the ranch house and sat down, looking out at the hills.

One of the boys should have stayed. But he was not worried. If an attack came he could stand them off for a good long while. He had protection and a good field of fire . . . but it would soon be dark.

The night came and held only silence. Above the towering black walls of the Gap the sky seemed light, and stars hung like lanterns in the still sky.

A wind came down the pass and sent leaves skittering over the hard-packed ground. He walked outside and went to the corrals. The horses seemed friendly and close. Restlessly, he walked back. It was early, but he might catch a bit of sleep.

He stretched out on a cot and stared up into the darkness. It semed unnaturally still, but he was tired. . . .

Suddenly, he was awake. How long he had slept he had no idea, but he came awake with a start, instantly aware of distant sound. A wagon rolling over stones. In the clear night air of the desert, channeled by the walls of the Gap, he caught the sound from some distance.

With Garry's Winchester in his hand he went outside to the gate. Standing at the corner of the stone chuckhouse, he strained his eyes into the darkness.

After a while he heard vague sounds. To a man who had fought Apaches and Kiowas, these men seemed clumsy. He listened, judging their distance and number.

Stepping around the corner of the bunkhouse he lit a cigar, took a deep draw, and placed it on the windowsill ready to hand.

He was alone but he was not worried. He had fought before, from worse positions. Like the time he and Red Jenkins had fought Comanches from a buffalo wallow. Or the time three hands from the old Goodnight outfit ran into a Kiowa war party. He chuckled, remembering. It would be like the old days.

A faint footfall sounded. Somebody was creeping up the Gap. He stepped around the corner and took another long draw on his cigar, then picked up the Winchester. When a footfall sounded again the rifle came smoothly to his shoulder and he fired.

Running a half dozen steps, he fired again, and sprang back for a third and fourth shot. He spaced his shots, shooting blindly down the Gap.

There was silence and then a stone rattled. He fired at the sound and heard a yelp, whether of pain or only astonishment he could not say, but instantly there was a volley.

He was standing behind the gate post and was completely sheltered. The sound of the shots racketed against the walls, and died away into dark silence. The Gap was still.

"Quite a party," he told himself. "Must be a dozen or more."

Something had been forcing itself upon his consciousness for some time, and suddenly he realized what it was. On the far wall of the Gap was a vague reflection, yet instantly he placed it.

The signal fire on Piety!

A warm feeling came over him and some of the loneliness vanished. The boys knew, and the boys were coming. Jud Devitt would pay for this night's work.

Down the Gap there was a faint stir. Instantly, he fired. He heard the bullet smack rock and ricochet, and a dozen rifles replied. Somewhere behind him hoofs pounded and then a horse raced down the Gap and a voice called out, "Hold it, Hank! It's me!"

Coffin swung down as a rifle shot, aimed at the voice, howled high and far.

"I lit the fire on Piety. The boys are comin'."

"How'd you know?"

"Saw 'em loading up. Couldn't find Shorty."

There was a long silence and Hank Rooney retrieved and relighted his cigar. In the shelter of the chuckhouse he smoked and waited.

"Hank . . . ?"

"Yeah?"

"Feller up there on the side-wall. He's tryin' to Injun us. How many times will he bounce?"

"He'll fall clean."

"Bet you a seegar. There's a boulder up there on that face."

"You got a bet."

The Winchester stabbed flame. They heard a grunting cry, a rattle of rocks, and the man fell. He hit ground solidly like a sack of flour.

"You owe me," Hank said.

Bullets screamed overhead and several smacked against the chuckhouse.

"Hey—where's Mahafee?"

"Aw, the old coot went back up the pass. He's got him a couple of wire traps. Tryin' to catch some quail. He ain't back."

Hank walked to the house and brought out the two Sharps rifles and the Spencer. Coffin was using his own Winchester.

Far up the pass behind them they heard the sound of horses. Neither man made a comment, but each had been listening, and each knew the boys were coming. Yet the first man to come into the yard came from Piety way. It was Clay Bell.

"Get set," Hank whispered suddenly. "They're fixin' to rush."

There was a sudden pound of running feet and a scramble of gravel. All three men opened up, firing low and fast. The rifles stabbed flame into the darkness and the acrid smell of gunpowder was in the air. Lead hailed around them, but the rush broke.

Even as they heard retreating feet, Jackson and Brown rode into the yard and sprang down, rifles in hand.

"Ain't over, is it?" Brown pleaded.

Mahafee came into the yard behind them. He said nothing, merely went into his kitchen and began to make coffee.

"Don't reckon they've quit," Rooney said, "but they lost their stomach for it."

Clay waited, listening. Out in the darkness he heard a faint groan.

Holding their rifles high for greater distance, all five men fired, their shots racketing down the Gap. Far down a man cried out, and someone cursed wickedly. Then there was silence.

"What's the matter?" Coffin yelled, tauntingly. "You boys leavin' so soon? We ain't had a chance to be hospitable yet!"

The echo died, and there was no other sound. The men waited, Hank Rooney smoking placidly.

"Light up, Hank," Clay said finally, "let's see what we've got."

Hank walked to the end of the prepared fuse and knelt. He drew deep on his cigar and the end glowed. He touched it to the fuse, which spluttered into flame that ate its way along. Suddenly the long piles of stacked brush burst into flame. In the bright light they could see three men lying upon the ground. One man had been trying to drag himself away, but when the brush burst into flame he held himself still.

"For Gawd's sake, don't shoot! We're through!"

Brown caught Bell's arm. "Listen!"

In the distance they could hear the sound of wagons. A yell came, then the sound of hoofs on stone and the rumble of wheels.

"Pullin' out," Brown said. He swore softly, bitterly. "Figured we'd have us a battle."

Bill Coffin spoke, his voice reflective. "As I recall, Devitt bought those broncs off Wheeler. Mighty skittish, they were."

The air was pregnant with speculation. "Mighty skittish," Jackson agreed, and in his voice was a sudden lighting of hope.

"He always maintained," Montana Brown said gravely, "they was the fastest runnin' teams in the country. You reckon he was right?"

"Interest of science," Coffin said, "maybe we should find out. You reckon?"

"Go ahead," Rooney suggested. "I'll see how bad those boys out there are hurt."

With a yell, the three cowhands ran for their horses and rode whooping into the night.

Rooney chuckled. "Man's only young once," he said to Clay. He drew on his cigar. "Boss, I reckon those horses will be the fastest runnin' teams in the country this night, anyway!"

Hank Rooney and Bell walked out to the fallen men. "If

you want to lie quiet and be taken care of," Rooney advised them, "don't start anything."

One man was dead . . . he was that one who had been shot off the rock wall by Coffin. One man had been shot through the leg, and the other shot twice through the shoulder. When they were bedded down in the bunkhouse and getting care from Rooney and coffee from Mahafee, Clay Bell walked back to the corral.

"Takin' the black," he told Hank. "I'm goin' into town. Shorty's alone."

An hour after he had gone, three weary and bedraggled punchers rode back into the ranch yard. Over their coffee they told gleefully of their race with the wagons.

"Them horses could run, all right," Jackson said. "Montana nicked one with a .45 and he suddenly recalled some relatives back in Texas an' lit a shuck."

"They might have made it," Coffin agreed, " 'cept the wagon tipped over."

"Runnin' yet, them horses."

A young lumberjack with a broken leg turned around on his bunk. "What happened to the jacks?"

"Walkin'," Coffin said.

Montana gulped coffee. "What'd you boys give us for twenty-two pairs of high lace boots?"

"You made 'em walk? In their sock feet? Hell, I'd rather have a busted leg!"

"They started for Tucson," Coffin said. "We figured they wouldn't have no reason to go to Tinkersville."

Quiet settled on the ranch. Jackson stood guard at the gate and was relieved by Coffin. Montana Brown, after a word with Rooney, saddled up and started for town. It was still dark—at least an hour before the first gray of dawn would light the sky.

Clay Bell had gone down the Gap, but turned off the trail and cut across country for Tinkersville. The black was restless and wanted to run but he held him in. There was no telling what might lie ahead, but he had little hope of any break, despite this new defeat for Devitt.

Stag Harvey and Kilburn were still in town. Was that entirely accident?

It would pay to have a care, for Devitt might not hesi-tate to hire them. There had been shooting, and if there was more, nobody would be surprised. So far Devitt had lost, but with Harvey and Kilburn at his side there would still be trouble. They were dangerous men, men who killed without a qualm, men reared to the gun and steeled and tempered in its use.

Bert Garry was dead and Shorty was in town. Much might have happened, but his first call had been to the ranch. Seriously, he pondered the situation.

He was not worried about Shorty. The man was cool and careful, and a thoroughly dangerous fighter. No gunman, he had served his time in several cattle wars, had fought Indians and had been over the trail. He was tough and salty, and a thinking man. He was no match for speed with Stag or Kilburn, but he was dangerous to either of them. He was a man who would have to be killed before he could be stopped.

And neither Kilburn nor Harvey were apt to take up the fight of a lumberjack.

The fact remained that for several hours Shorty had been in town alone, and that town was filled with enemies.

Clay Bell saw the sharp-cut outlines of roofs against the sky. Few lights showed at this hour, and everything was quiet.

Somewhere a rooster crowed . . . another light went out. Clay Bell rode on, the only sound the footfalls of his horse on the dusty road.

CHAPTER 16

WHEN CLAY BELL rode out of town headed for his ranch at Emigrant Gap, it was Sam Tinker who brought up the subject of the grazing rights.

"The rights to graze that area, along with the sole rights to develop or improve that land, belong to Clay," Tibbott said. "Chase tried to block me, and he was making trouble until I met a man named O'Connell. Seems Bell saved his life at Shiloh.

"O'Connell is active in the Party, and he knows the right people. On Clay's right of prior use, the fact that he's kept a fire watch, and that he has sold beef to the Army all helped.

"O'Connell turned up a quartermaster who convinced the Senate committee that Bell's beef was needed right there, that in case of a new Apache outbreak it would be the only stable source of supply in that area. We stretched a point here and there, but we made it stick."

There was silence in the dining room. Tinker's spoon rattled on his saucer.

"Leaves Devitt without a leg to stand on," Miller said. "He won't like it."

"Nor will some others," Tinker said grimly.

The big clock ticked off the seconds, and they waited, listening. Nobody phrased the situation, yet all understood. Somewhere out in the town was Shorty Jones, and somewhere else was Pious Pete Simmons.

It was dark and still out there . . . and at any minute a man could die.

Miller walked to the door and stood outside for some time. Finally he came in. "Firing at the Gap," he said.

"They won't get through."

Bob Tripp was dead tired but he could not sleep. He had watched the men load up for the drive to the Gap, then he had gone back inside. This was something of which he wanted no part. Many of the lumberjacks had done some hunting, a few of them had served in the Army, but most of them were men unskilled at fighting, and from talk around town Tripp knew they were facing a salty lot of fighting men.

Bob Tripp was no coward, and he was also not a fool. Anyway, he had orders to stay in town.

Jud Devitt had lost his head. It was sheer insanity to send that bunch out there to tackle the curly wolves from the high country who worked for Bell.

Boots scraped on the gravel outside and a light tap came on the door.

"Who's there?"

"Williams. Open up."

Tripp unbarred the door and Williams slid into the room. His face was drawn and white. "Bob, that kid died a while ago. Jones is packin' a gun for Simmons!"

"Didn't Simmons go to the Gap?"

"The Boss kept him here."

Williams mopped his face, then tucked the bandana in his pocket. "Bob, I'm leavin'. I'll fight, but I'm no killer, and I don't cotton to the ways of Duval and Simmons. Nor Jud Devitt, either, for that matter."

Bob Tripp sat down on his cot and began to pull on his boots. When he had tied the laces he sat there, staring at the gray rectangle that was the window. The room itself was in total darkness. Suddenly he reached under the cot and pulled out a carpetbag. He began to take down clothes and stuff them into it.

"There's a train at daylight, Wat. I'll go with you."

"We can wait in the brush across the tracks," Williams said.

It was Jim Narrows who told Pete Simmons about Garry's death.

The burly Simmons was more the thug than the lumberjack. He had found occasion to shove Narrows around and had enjoyed taunting the older man. Jim Narrows was not a vindictive man, but neither was he a man likely to forget. When he heard that Bert Garry was dead he had deliberately walked by the shack where Simmons and Duval bunked. Duval had led the attack on the Gap, and Simmons was alone.

Pious Pete was smoking on the step when Narrows came along. "Evenin', Simmons."

"Who is it?"

"Narrows. Just came from the Tinker House."

"What's up? Seems a lot of stirrin' around?"

"You're a dead man, Pete."

Jim Narrows said it quietly, without emotion. He could almost feel sorry for the man, but he remembered how he had put the boots to Bert Garry. He had seen what those calks could do to a man's face.

"Huh?"

Jim too his time. He lighted his pipe. "Pete, that kid died tonight."

"Garry?" Simmons was on his feet.

"You'd better get a gun, Pete." Narrows spoke quietly. "When Shorty Jones heard that Garry was dead he just turned and walked out. He's lookin' for you, Pete."

Simmons turned and blundered through the door.

"Better not strike a light," Narrows advised. "That would only hurry it."

Jim Narrows walked away down the little slope. There was little time left for Pete. Knowing Shorty Jones, Narrows had no doubt of the outcome. Bert Garry had been a fine lad, but it was never good to see a man frightened.

Pete Simmons strapped on a six-gun and picked up a shotgun. He went down the alley, hesitated at the street, then crossed to the livery barn.

A solitary light glowed over the door of the stable and there was nobody in sight. For a long while Simmons studied that street; then he crossed swiftly. It was past one in the morning and nobody was around. Even the hostler was asleep.

Simmons got a horse and saddled him clumsily, then led him to the door. Dropping the bridle reins, he stepped into the light to look down the street.

As he appeared in the light he heard a boot scrape on

gravel. He stiffened, standing where he was, his mouth dry, his heart pounding heavily.

"You took your time, Pete."

Simmons' last vestige of fighting courage surfaced. "I ain't running!"

"Goin' for a ride, then? Didn't figured you was the type to ride under the stars, Pete."

Simmons held the shotgun but the muzzle was down. He wished it was higher. He wondered how long it would take to come level. And just where was Shorty? Simmons strained his eyes at the shadow. There was a line of something darker—was that Shorty?

There would be little time. A fraction of a second, only. He would have to swing the gun up. Suppose his finger missed the trigger guard?

"The kid never wanted trouble, Pete. We didn't even know there was a fight on. We had just come in for a drink. We'd been ridin' dusty, all day."

Shorty Jones' voice sounded nearer. "He was a good kid, Pete. It ain't good to see the life stomped from a boy like that. Even up, it might have been different. You ganged us."

"It was orders!" Simmons' throat was hoarse. His eyes probed the darkness, not quite sure.

"You'll never stomp another man, Pete—not ever."

Simmons' lips felt parched. He could do with a drink. Where was Shorty? He took a firmer grip on the shotgun. His palm was sweaty—suppose the gun slipped?

Something seemed to move in the darkness and Pete Simmons' nerve broke. He sprang aside and swung up with the shotgun. His finger groped for a trigger but got both at once, and the shotgun roared and jumped in his hands.

The darkness was deceiving and he was frightened. He sprang back and, dropping the shotgun, groped for his pistol.

Shorty Jones stepped into the half-light. The post near him had taken most of the blast. A few shots had hit him and a thin trickle of blood showed on his cheek.

"Good-bye, Pete."

Shorty fired twice, lifting his gun and taking his time, the two staccato reports blending. Simmons shrugged high his shoulders and rose on his tiptoes, then fell.

Shorty Jones looked down at the man, waiting carefully. Simmons shuddered, slowly his muscles subsided, and he was dead.

Shorty thumbed cartridges into empty chambers and holstered his gun. He turned and walked slowly back up the street. When he was almost at the Tinker House he stopped to roll a smoke. He did not look back.

In the dining room of the Tinker House men sat huddled over their coffee. They heard the heavy boom of the shotgun, then the two sharp, deliberate shots.

In his office down the street Jud Devitt had heard those shots too. Now he sat across the desk from two men.

"Things have changed," Harvey said.

"We don't like it," Kilburn added.

"Who fired those shots?" Devitt asked irritably. "Who was that? I thought it was you."

"It was Jones. He killed Pete Simmons."

Jud Devitt compressed his lips. Another mark against Clay Bell. He felt angry and uneasy. Nothing seemed to be going right. This town was a jinx, everything had gone wrong here, in a stupid hick cattle town!

"What do you mean—things have changed?"

"We took on a job. It looked pretty good. Now it doesn't look good any more."

"You're quitting?" Devitt sneered.

Stag Harvey shook his head. "Call it what you like. This here's our business. We don't like to lose. You've lost."

Jud Devitt was suddenly cold and angry. "Don't talk like fools!" he said. "I've not lost! I can't lose! My man in Washington—"

"Hardy Tibbott came back today. Tonight. He's been in Washington. Clay Bell got the grazing right secured for ten years."

So that was how a dream ended? A beautiful, fool-proof plan. This timber, so close to Mexican Central's main line that transportation was a minor item. He could bid far below the others and still make a rich profit. And now it was over. If Tibbott had come back with the grazing permit then it was ended. Even if his men broke into the Deep Creek range, he was finished.

And all because of one man.

He looked up from his desk. "All right," Devitt said, "I'll make it five thousand dollars if he is dead before sundown tomorrow."

"No."

Jack Kilburn shifted his feet and Stag looked at him. Kilburn spread his hands, and Harvey knew what he meant. They were broke.

"Five thousand." Devitt repeated the sum. "I have it here."

Stag Harvey looked down at his hands. He had never deliberately gone in for killing. Fighting, yes. Yet he had always known, he realized now, that it would end this way. That if he continued to use a gun he would end by doing this. And Clay Bell was a good man.

A little chill struck him, remembering Bell. There was something about gunfighters, one always knew another.

"Half of it now," he said. "On the line."

"All right. The other half when the job is done."

Devitt opened his safe and took out a sheaf of bills. He counted them out on the desk-top.

"Don't worry about the rest. I'll pay it."

Jack Kilburn looked up at Devitt and something inside Jud turned over slowly, sickeningly.

"We ain't worried, Devitt. We'll collect."

Stag Harvey got to his feet and Kilburn followed suit. "Have the rest of it on you, Devitt. We'll want it fast."

Outside, they walked away from the house before they paused.

"Wonder if he knows what'll happen to him when Bell is killed?"

"No," Kilburn said thoughtfully, "I don't think he's thought about that."

"Simmons is dead."

"But Devitt don't read the sign."

They walked down to the main street, then stopped

again. "We'd better get some sleep, Jack. I don't like this. Not a bit."

Jud Devitt sat alone behind his desk. For a moment he stared down at his hands with a feeling of something like revulsion. All the details of the last few minutes seemed dreamlike and unreal. He had actually bought a man's death. Legally, he was a murderer.

But this was war . . . it was a war in which all the rules were changed. It was not in Jud Devitt to go in for self-analysis, nor to realize that this was a war of his own making, a war which he had declared and in which he had opened hostilities. He was a man who meant to win. The admired man was the go-getter, the man who did things. Devitt was not one to stop to consider the rights and wrongs of what he did, nor to realize there is a fine line one may not cross.

The feeling of doubt and revulsion passed. Bell had his grazing permit, but tomorrow that permit would be revoked by his death. He had no heirs. Within a brief time the hands who worked for Bell would drift away, the land would lie idle, and he could walk in and take over.

What had become of Tripp? Suddenly irritable, he wanted his labor foreman, but the man was not around. Angrily, he looked at his watch, and for the first time realized that he had sat up most of the night. It would be morning soon.

He heard voices, someone passing in the street. He paused by the window, his light out, listening.

When he turned away he walked to his cot and pulled off his boots. Then for a long time he sat there. Shorty Jones had killed Pete Simmons—two shots centered in his shirt pocket at a distance of thirty feet.

CHAPTER 17

DAYLIGHT WAS streaming in the window when Clay Bell awakened. For a long time he lay still, assembling his thoughts and putting the pieces of the picture in their places.

Simmons was dead. Shorty Jones had hunted down the man who had crippled Bert Garry and caused the young cowboy's death.

Simmons had mistaken the heavy post near which Jones stood for the puncher himself. A few of the buckshot had clipped Shorty, but a scratched cheek and arm were his only injuries.

This morning there were few lumberjacks around, and most of them were silent and kept in tight groups. The boisterous talk and rough horse-play of the past days was missing.

Those who had been started from the trail to Emigrant Gap in their sock feet had not returned to Tinkersville. Several others had left by the early train, Bob Tripp and Williams among them.

Yet there was a noticeable tension in the town. Looking from the second-story hotel window, Bell could sense it in the way people moved, in the very quiet of the town. Men had been killed, and there might be more killing yet to come. Tinkersville was unsure and was taking no chances.

Clay splashed water on his chest and shoulders, and combed his hair. When he was dressed, he brushed his boots carefully, then checked his guns. He swung the belts around his hips, and settled the guns in their places.

He felt a curious reluctance to leave his room, and was puzzled by it. Finally, he opened the door and stepped out into the hall. A careful man always, he stopped there and looked up and down the corridor. The doors were closed. There was no sign of movement.

At the head of the stairs he hesitated and turned and

looked back down the hall again. Then he descended, casually, but with eyes alert. Jud Devitt was still in town, and
Jud could be dangerous.

He had seen no sign of Morton Schwabe. Tibbott's arrival and his broadcasting of the news that Bell had won his
grazing permit would probably stop any move that
Schwabe might make. But remembering Kesterson's story
of Schwabe buying shells, it was not a good idea to gamble.

Ed Miller looked up from his inevitable ledger. "You're
late," he said grinning. "She's already gone in."

Clay walked past the desk and into the dining room.
Judge Riley was there, talking with Sam Tinker. Kesterson
sat near by, and alone. There was no sign of either Devitt
or Noble Wheeler. Colleen sat at a table alone and, after
hanging up his hat, Clay sat down across from her.

She was pale this morning and her eyes seemed unnaturally large.

"You're up early," he said.

"I couldn't sleep—and then those shots."

"It was Shorty."

"I know. Father went down."

They were silent, waiting until the waitress had cleared
away dishes left by Judge Riley and brought coffee to Clay.

"Is it over now?"

He shook his head. "You know it isn't. It won't be until
Jud leaves town."

"Maybe if I went to see him?"

"Don't go. Nothing will make him leave until he makes
up his own mind. But most of his crowd are gone."

He tried his coffee. "Mind if I smoke?"

"Please do." She looked up suddenly. "Clay, why don't
you go back to the ranch? He won't be here long, and if
you stay, there'll be trouble."

"I can't run away from a fight."

Her father had told her this. Masculine pride . . . but
something more. A man must be respected by those of his
community, and in this country, where fighting courage
and skill were respected social virtues, he could not leave.

Too long had these people lived by the gun. These men
and women had crossed the plains, they had fought In-

dians and outlaws, and they had built homes where it took strength to build and courage to fight—and the willingness to fight was still a social virtue of the first order. The town was not yet tame.

All those in the dining room were talking about the events of the night. Colleen sat quietly, watching Clay eat. A month ago she would have been horrified at things she now accepted.

This man had killed men. He was fighting a war just as deadly as any war with flags and uniforms, and a war that must be won. Remembering the hours she had sat with Bert Garry, she knew they had been good hours for her. Bert had been conscious and aware much of the time. He had talked and she had listened; she had heard his slow stories of the work on the B-Bar, how good Clay was to work for, how patiently he built his herds, how solidly he planned.

Now Bert Garry was dead, and the man who had actually killed him was dead. But the man responsible was still alive and still in town.

She felt curiously drawn to this tall, quiet young man across the table. Time and again she had tried to understand it, but her feelings defied analysis. When she was with him she felt right. When she was away from him she thought of their brief minutes together and wondered when she would see him again. From the first there had been an unspoken understanding.

Shorty Jones came in. She heard the door close and looked around, following Clay's quick glance. Shorty wore a sun-faded checked shirt and jeans. He had his gun tied down. His broad face was red from the sun, and his corn-silk brows shadowed his eyes. He walked quickly to the table and stopped, hat in hand.

"Clay, I got to talk to you."

"Is there trouble at the Gap?"

"Not now—that bunch that jumped the ranch are gone. Buck Chalmers came in few minutes back. Told me they got themselves a ride toward Tucson with some freighters."

"Had breakfast?"

"Sure." Shorty hesitated, not certain how to say what he had in mind.

"Boss," he said suddenly, "after that Simmons shootin' I scouted around some, huntin' for Duval. He must've gone to the Gap with that crowd because I didn't find him. But I saw somethin' else."

"What?"

"I saw Stag Harvey and Jack Kilburn comin' out of Jud Devitt's office at two in the mornin'. They had a lot of money they were splittin'."

So there it was.

All along Clay had feared this would happen. Devitt was a man who did not know how to lose, he could not bear to lose. Now, driven into a corner, he was buying a killing. Yet how far a step was that from the beating Simmons and Duval had given Bert Garry?

"Shorty, how about you sitting down over there with a cup of coffee? Sort of keep your eyes open?"

Shorty nodded assent and moved to the seat from which the approach to the hotel could be watched.

Colleen put her hand over Clay's. "Clay . . . what is it? What does it mean?"

Harvey and Kilburn might be sure-thing operators but not dry-gulchers. They would meet him in the street or out on the plains, but it would be a man-to-man operation with an even break all around—as much as one man could get from two. At least, he would see who was shooting and he would have his chance to shoot back. But these men were past-masters of guncraft. They would choose the time, and they would arrange the situation to put him in a tactically bad position.

"I've been told about those men, Clay. What does it mean? You can tell me."

He looked up from his plate and directly at her. "Yes, Colleen, I think I can tell you. I think I can tell you anything. I think you're a woman who would walk beside a man. I think you've got nerve."

He took a swallow of coffee, then put down his cup. "Harvey and Kilburn hire their guns. They are tough, dangerous men. Harvey and me have always sort of walked circles around each other. Kilburn, he don't like me much. But they fight as a team."

"You think Jud hired them—to kill you?"

"Would he?"

She sat very still, measuring what she knew of the man. His quick, hard decisions, his ruthlessness, his arrogant resentment of failure. He had a love of doing big jobs quickly, a love of winning. Victory to him was a compelling necessity.

It must have seemed a very simple thing to a man of his ability and his confidence to come into a town like Tinkersville and log off the Deep Creek range. It was a much smaller job than many he had undertaken, and one that must have seemed to offer no obstacles. He had been brusque and confident and sure . . . and then he had met defeat at every point.

Clay Bell had not been frightened by his usual aggressive tactics. He had not been bluffed, and he had met Jud Devitt's attempts at every point and had beaten him. Devitt's effort to frighten the B-Bar by having two of their men beaten had backfired. It had not left them short-handed enough, and it had not stopped them.

She remembered Jud Devitt from back east. Well-dressed, confident, very sure of himself and disdainful of others. He had seemed a big man there, a man who got things done, the sort of a man whom everyone admired. Girls had envied her, for beside him their men seemed insipid and tame.

In the days that followed her arrival in Tinkersville she had seen his brusque confidence take a rude shock. She had seen hard lines at the corners of his mouth, had seen him irritable and even brutal. She had seen the true nature of the man emerge. He was a man thoughtless of others, despising all but himself, riding roughshod over personalities and feelings.

She looked up at Clay.

"Yes, Clay, I believe he would. He can't take defeat. He isn't big enough. He can't even admit it." She hesitated, suddenly aware of the sensitiveness of the man she faced, of his thoughtfulness, of . . .

"Clay, what will you do?"

"Why," he made up his mind even as he replied, "I'll go see Stag and ask him about it."

She started to protest and he grinned at her suddenly. "Now don't start acting like a wife!"

Something inside her seemed to catch and hold itself very still. She seemed suddenly short of breath, and she looked up at him and for a long moment their eyes held across the table.

"Save it," he said quietly, "for other times, later. I've been thinking about that, you know."

"So have I."

Had she? Suddenly she knew it had been there, between them, every second of the time. Even when they were not together.

"I'm not going to wait for them to set it up," he told her. "I'm going to meet them halfway. I'll have to, if I want to live."

He stood up and leaning suddenly across the table he kissed her on the lips. Then he straightened, the action so smooth and easy that it had gone unnoticed in the dining room.

The door opened and a lean, brown man stepped inside. He wore a brown beaver sombrero and a brown vest, and his face was long and tanned. His legs were slightly bowed and he wore two guns, tied down.

It was Montana Brown. "Boss, I hear talk around. If it's to be Harvey and Kilburn, I want in."

Shorty Jones started to protest.

"He's right, Shorty. Montana had a run-in with Kilburn once . . . besides, you had your action last night."

"Kilburn an' me," Montana said, "we got it to settle."

"All right." Clay put a hand on Brown's shoulder. "We'll do it this way . . ." Quickly and concisely he outlined his plan, and Montana nodded agreement as he listened.

"You," he turned to Shorty, "locate Devitt and keep an eye on him. Don't make a move unless he tries to cut in. If he does, he's your meat."

Rush Jackson, Hank Rooney, and Bill Coffin rode into

town shortly before noon and went to the bar at the Home-stake. With sure instinct, they knew the showdown was at hand. Jones met them and apprised them of the situation here. The men who had been watching cattle were down at the ranch and were keeping an eye on both the Gap and The Notch.

It was still and warm. The sky was bare of clouds, the dust gathered heat, the unpainted, gray, false-fronted buildings reflected it. Over the desert, heat waves rippled and danced between the eye and the faraway hills. Somewhere out there a faint plume of dust lifted.

In his office at the bank Noble Wheeler sat before his worn desk, his fat face shadowed and dark with worry. He knew as well as did the others that a showdown was coming. His own part in it he did not know.

Sam Tinker moved to his chair on the porch of the hotel. Judge Riley went up to his room and took off his coat. Seated at his desk in shirt and suspenders, he began a letter to go back east. There was no sound in the street. Occasionally a rig rattled through, or a horse stamped. Once or twice he heard voices, and once, laughter. These only served to emphasize the stillness of the town. It lay quiet, poised, and waiting . . . .

Jud Devitt got up from his desk. His shirt was stained with sweat from where he had been lying on the divan a while before. There were circles of sweat under his arms. He mopped his face and swore softly. He had not shaved, but this morning he was scarcely conscious of it. His face was drawn, his eyes hollow.

Why the devil didn't they get it over with! Anger stirred him . . . was it so complicated to shoot a man?

He looked out the window.

Down the street a man sat in the shade of an adobe, his hat pulled low over his eyes. He was smoking, and he wore a gun. It was Shorty Jones.

Jud Devitt drew back from the window, his mouth suddenly dry. Jones had killed Pete Simmons last night. What did he want here now?

CHAPTER 18

R USH JACKSON came up the street and into the hotel. He paused beside Clay. "Saw Stag down at the station, buyin' a ticket."

"Maybe he's goin' to grab his soogan and run," Montana suggested, then shook his head. "Ain't like him."

Bell weighed the idea. He knew that Harvey and Kilburn needed money, and neither man was the sort to dodge a fight when it offered cash on the line.

"No," he said finally, "they've seen you boys in town. They'll make their play, then hit the train running."

"Then we can figure the time," Brown said thoughtfully. "They'll make their try just before train time."

Ed Miller was listening. "This is Saturday. Three trains today. One comes through about three this afternoon."

About three . . .

The morning drew on and the sun was warmer. There was no sign of Devitt. Shorty Jones loafed in the shadows, moving with them. The slivery gray boards of the walks grew hot. Montana walked to the pitcher and poured a glass of water. The street was almost empty.

A rig came in from the south. It stood a moment in the street while the driver went into Kesterson's and hurried out again. He jumped into the rig, whirled it around the corner and out of the street.

No horses stood at the hitch rails. The few people whose business took them to the stores made hurried purchases and went home. Others stayed within doors, yet a good many were around.

Clay Bell went to his room and slipped out of his boots and gun belts, placing the guns close at hand on a chair by the bed. Heavy with weariness, he dozed off, awakened, then slept.

In his office Jud Devitt paced the floor, swearing. Remembering, he went to his safe and counted out twenty-five hundred dollars. About to return the black box to the safe, he hesitated, struck by some vague feeling of caution. There was not much left, but ...

Suddenly, he stuffed the rest of the money in his pockets, returning the empty box to the safe and locking the door. Then he went to the window and looked out. Jones was hunched beside the building, smoking.

Devitt took the twenty-five hundred dollars and stuffed it into a small canvas sack.

Sam Tinker had been thinking, and he was a man who made his decisions slowly and with great care. He put down his pipe and heaved himself from his chair. Then he lumbered down the steps and across the street to the bank.

Noble Wheeler sat behind his scarred desk, waiting. The door opened and Sam Tinker came in. He did not sit down. Sam Tinker was a big man, and when he stood like that he looked enormous and awe-inspiring. He mopped his face with a blue bandana, then stuffed it into his pocket.

"Noble," he said, "I started this here town, an' she bears my name. I like her. She's had her ups and downs, but she's been a fair to middlin' place to live. I aim to keep her so."

"Why, sure." Wheeler sounded puzzled. "What can I do to help?"

Sam Tinker mopped his face again. "You can leave town."

"What? What did you say?"

"There's a three o'clock train on Saturday an' you'll close the bank now. I want folks' money left here for 'em. That will give you time to pack. You take that train, an' we don't never want to see you no more."

Wheeler's face flushed, then paled. "Have you gone crazy, Tinker? What sort of talk is that?"

"I said my say. You be on that three o'clock train. Just about that time Stag Harvey and his partner will try to kill Bell. Devitt put 'em up to it."

"What's that got to do with me?"

Sam Tinker looked at him unpleasantly. He disliked a traitor and he disliked a coward. Noble Wheeler was both.

Coolly, he enumerated the things Wheeler had done. He had brought Devitt to town. He had refused Bell a loan. He had tried to get an old charge raised against Brown, and he had tried to kill Clay Bell.

"Who says that?" Wheeler was both angry and frightened.

"Clay trailed you—that boy could trail a quail across a salt flat. When he finishes with Harvey he'll come lookin', or his boys will."

Noble Wheeler sat very still. He looked down at the desk and at his hands. He looked around the dingy little office, at the fly-specked windows. His fat lips worked and twisted with wordless protest.

Then he threw his hands wide. "But—this is my business! It's all I've got in the world!"

Sam Tinker did not reply. Grimly, he stood waiting. The thought of the B-Bar hands went wildly through Wheeler's mind.

He remembered the body of Pete Simmons, lying bloody and dirty before the livery stable door, the horse he had hoped to ride standing ground-hitched near by. He remembered the body of the man the B-Bar men had brought in from the ranch, the other men who had been merely wounded. He remembered Montana Brown's lean hatchet face, and the hard impudence of Bill Coffin. He licked his lips.

"You came into town with mighty little money," Sam Tinker was ruthless. "You made some here. You leave with what you got on you."

"That's robbery! That's—"

"You goin'?" Sam's voice was deceptively mild. Noble Wheeler looked up and did not like what he saw. Sam Tinker had come into this country when the Apaches held it. He had outlasted them.

"I—I'm goin'."

His hands fluttered helplessly. Then he saw the gun in the drawer, and suddenly something stilled inside him. He had never killed, but . . . He looked up and saw that Sam Tinker held a tiny .41 derringer in his hand.

CHAPTER 19

A T TWENTY-FIVE minutes past two Clay Bell came down the stairs from his room and ordered a cup of coffee in the dining room.

He sat very still at the table, thinking over his plans. He flexed the fingers of his right hand and tentatively moved his shoulder. His hand was no longer stiff and he felt good. The rugged life and good food of the cattle country had brought him out of the weakness left by his wound.

He drank his coffee slowly, and when the cup was half empty, he rolled a smoke. When he was lighting up, the door opened and Jackson came in.

"Stag's down at the livery barn. Kilburn's nowheres in sight."

"Thanks."

"If Stag comes up the street you'll have the sun in your eyes."

"I thought of that."

As he smoked he considered the situation. Jud Devitt could be considered as out of the picture for the duration of the fight. Shorty was watching him, and Shorty was no man to fool with.

Mentally, he surveyed the walk from the livery barn, timing Stag. He knew that Harvey was the planner, that he would have calculated the killing with cold-blooded accuracy. Kilburn would be spotted where he could be of most help.

He turned suddenly and looked at Coffin, who had come into the room.

"Bill, a few days ago I saw you aping my walk. Could you do it again?"

Coffin flushed sheepishly at the accusation, but at the question his eyes sharpened.

"I reckon," he said slowly.

"Then switch hats with me."

Bill Coffin looked briefly into Clay's eyes, then exchanged hats.

Colleen came down the steps and looked across the room toward him, yet instinctively she knew this was no time for her to approach him. She walked across the room to her father and sat down there with him.

Clay got to his feet and settled his guns in place. With Coffin he walked to the door, where they conversed in low tones, then Clay turned and left Coffin standing at the door. He walked back through the room and as he passed Colleen he dropped his hand to her shoulder and squeezed gently. Then he went on, without speaking.

When he was gone there was silence in the room. Sam Tinker could feel the sweat on his face. His mouth felt dry. He looked at Coffin standing in the door, his back toward the room. The blond cowhand was smoking a cigarette.

Somewhere a dog yelped . . . then there was silence. The town seemed to be without movement. Far across the hills, a train whistle sounded. It was still miles away.

Judge Riley cleared his throat and looked across at Colleen. Neither spoke.

A spoon rattled on a saucer and someone gasped and turned, half in irritation. The slight rustle of the man's clothing was loud in the stillness.

Stag Harvey had planned well. Jack Kilburn was posted in an empty building between the blacksmith shop and the Piddle Saddle Works.

Harvey pulled his hat brim low and stepped out into the street, and as he did so he saw the tall, black-hatted figure in a gray wool shirt and black neckerchief step from the Tinker House.

Stag Harvey felt a curious elation. This was as it should be. No ducking, no dodging, two men meeting as men should meet. Killer he might be, but he was a product of the Code Duello.

The man up the street walked to the center of the thoroughfare and did an abrupt left face, looking down street, the sun in his eyes.

Stag Harvey started to move, a glow of satisfaction going through him. He walked on, taking his time and judging his pace and that of the man coming toward him so they would finally have their showdown with the Piddle Saddle Works at right angles to Bell.

The distance narrowed. Stag felt sweat on his cheeks. A dust-devil spun crazily in the street and played itself out against the steps of a building up ahead. Little puffs of dust lifted from his boots as he stepped off the distance.

A fleeting black shadow passed over the street and involuntarily Stag glanced up.

A buzzard . . .

He felt a faint chill, then his eyes came to focus on the man before him. He stopped dead still. There was something odd about . . . Why, that wasn't—

"Stag!"

Clay Bell's voice rang clear and unmistakable in the empty, sunlit street.

"You looking for me?"

The voice was behind on his right. Stag Harvey wheeled, drawing as he turned, but even as he drew he realized he had been outmaneuvered. Jack Kilburn was now behind him and out of the play!

Clay had stepped from between the buildings, and as Stag turned, Clay Bell palmed his guns.

He stood very straight in the street and his right-hand gun came up. Looking across the distance into the blazing gray eyes of the killer, he began to fire.

The sound of his gun was like a roll of drums in the narrow street, the sound rolling back from the false-fronted buildings. Flame spouted at him from Harvey's guns, but Stag jerked suddenly as if by a hidden wire and on his shoulder there was a blotch of blood that had not been there before.

Clay walked forward, the acrid smell of gunsmoke and street dust in his nostrils. The hammers slipped under his thumbs as he fired. He saw Stag back up through a blur of smoke and he fired again, then shifted guns as Harvey went to his knees.

But Harvey came up and started on a stumbling run

toward the Homestake, feeding shells into his gun. In the silence following the roll of guns, Clay Bell could hear the gunman panting hoarsely.

He felt cold and steady. The instant was sharp with clarity. He fired again, but the man turned and Clay knew it was a clean miss. Spreading his feet apart he heard a sound of firing from up the street, but he did not turn his eyes from the weaving figure of Harvey.

Before shifting guns he had fired twice from his left-hand gun. Two shells left . . .

Feet apart, he lifted the gun. Stag was blood to the waist, his face haggard, but his eyes seemed blazing with an unholy fire. Stag's gun came up and Clay fired. His bullet struck Stag under his uplifted arm and came out his back.

Stag's gun slipped from his fingers, and using his right hand he reached over and took the left-hand gun from an arm that would no longer support it.

One bullet left, Clay Bell waited, not wanting to shoot again.

"Drop it, Stag! You're done!"

The man was dying on his feet, but reason no longer lived behind his eyes. The last thought within that brain was the thought to kill. The brain willed the hand and the gun lifted. Through the gunsmoke and the fog that was beginning to cloud his eyes, Stag Harvey attempted to fire one more time.

Grim and bloody, weaving on his feet, blood darkening his jeans, he painstakingly got the gun into position.

"Drop it, Stag! You're too good a man to die doing another man's dirty work!"

He held his fire, knowing he could place the bullet where he wanted it now.

There was no need. The gun slipped suddenly, too heavy for the gunman's hand. Teetering, with all the slowness and patience of a man very drunk, Stag Harvey stooped to reach for the gun. And when he stooped he fell headlong.

Clay crossed to him and kicked the gun away. Harvey's

eyes were glazing, but as Clay stepped into his line of vision they seemed to clear.

"Clay"—he gasped the words hoarsely—"this here's a—hell of a way to make—to make a—a livin'!"

People crowded forward. Bell looked around. "Get Doc McClean!"

"He's with Montana," Shorty Jones said. "He caught a slug. Not too bad."

"Kilburn?"

"Shot to doll rags."

Hank Rooney had knelt beside Harvey. He got to his feet. "You won't need a doctor here," he said. "He's gone."

Clay Bell turned away. Surprisingly, he was unhurt. His first shot had turned Harvey, and the gunman had never got lined up again. Men waited, listening for the word they expected. Finally Coffin put it into words. "What about Devitt? He hired these killers."

The train whistled.

Sam Tinker glanced up the street. On the platform Noble Wheeler would be waiting, ticket in hand.

"Let Devitt alone," Bell said. "I'll talk to him, myself."

"Schwabe came to town," Tinker said. "He saw what was happening an' he turned right around and rode out."

"He was encouraged," Rooney said. "Rush Jackson an' me—we sort of showed him the error of his ways. We figured he had him a choice . . . He didn't like it much."

Clay Bell unbuckled his gun belts. He handed them to Coffin.

"Without a gun?" Shorty was unbelieving.

"His way," Clay said quietly. "Fists are his style. He made his brag."

He turned abruptly, lifting his eyes over the heads of the crowd to the girl on the walk. Their eyes met.

"I'll be waiting," she said, and over the babble of voices he heard the words as if no others were spoken.

He lifted his hand to his hat, and then he turned and walked up the street.

CHAPTER 20

ALONE IN his office, Jud Devitt heard the sound of guns, the sound of the guns with which he bought death.

It was a strange sensation. Despite his arrogance and brutality of method, Jud Devitt might be called a civilized man. A month before, had it been suggested that he would have paid men to kill, he would have regarded the speaker as insane. Yet now, when he heard the sound of the guns, he felt a curious sensation of power, of triumph.

He had won! His fingers trembled as they rubbed his unshaven jaws.

It was over then. . . . And the man who had fought him, who had dared to fight him, that man was dead.

There was no place in the thinking of Jud Devitt for the possibility of one man defeating two, or of Clay Bell's escape. He possessed that curious respect for guns often owned by men who have not used them against other men. He did not know how easy it is for even an expert marksman to miss. Nor did he guess what an amazing amount of lead a human body can absorb without dying, or even falling.

He had been resisted. One of his men—no, more than one—had been killed. His wagons had been upset, his donkey engine and sawmill burned. But he had won. Defeat was behind him then.

He got out the remaining twenty-five hundred dollars and placed it upon the desk.

So little money! Twice that pile, and a man was dead. Wiped out—and all he stood for.

Jud Devitt was not a psychologist. He was a brusque and, he believed, an efficient man. He was a practical man, with no thought for the evolution or the degeneration of character. He thought, in this moment of triumph, only of victory. It was not in him to think back over the steps that had brought him to buying a man's death. Nor did he think of what that implied. Had he thought of it at all, he would have believed that he was as he had always been.

It was quiet in the little office. Sweat trickled along his jaws. His hair was rumpled from the hundred and more times that he had run nervous fingers through it. His face was unshaven, but he did not think of that. His shirt was sweat-stained and should be changed, but he, the carefully dressed and groomed, gave it no thought.

He had won—and if the death of one man might be bought, another might.

He would pay Harvey and Kilburn. He would put them on salary. He would retain them. Such men were valuable.

The world was made for the strong, the ruthless. It was made for kings—these others, they were peasants. Little men standing in the way of progress. Jud Devitt did not think that progress is built upon the efforts of many men, all working toward a goal.

He was not a drinking man, but now he got out the bottle and poured a drink into his water glass. He tossed it off, but the whiskey scarcely touched him. He was drinking the wine of victory, so intoxicating that mere alcohol could not affect him.

He put down the glass and sat back in his chair. He would get a new office. The logging would take months. Then he would make plans. East was the place, East was the place he should go, but before that there would be other battles to win out here.

He got to his feet again and thrust his hands into his pockets. Outside there was a distant muffle of sound, but it did not cut into his consciousness. No more than did the train whistle that had sounded a few minutes ago. The whistle had escaped his ears, lost somewhere in the welter of thoughts forcing themselves upon him in his moment of victory.

Jud Devitt walked to the window and looked out toward Deep Creek. He would wait three—no, two days. That would be sufficient. If the B-Bar riders had not packed and gone then, he would drive them off.

Dropping into his chair, he began to figure. Suppose he doubled his crew? Suppose he moved in a hundred men?

He could clear that piece off rapidly, fulfill his contract
and go on to something else.

Wait . . . .

Wheeler had something on his mind . . . find out. He
wrote that down. Find out about Wheeler.

First, to get Bob Tripp . . . For the first time then Jud
Devitt began to wonder. Where was Bob Tripp?

Tripp should be here, enjoying this moment. Come to
think of it, he had not seen him in hours. No matter . . .
Tripp was probably already making plans. He was probably wiring for a new and bigger crew.

The mutter of voices forced itself upon him. Someone
coming—a crowd, a mob.

Suddenly, he was frightened. Suppose . . . People in
this jerkwater town had liked Bell. Suppose they were
coming to hang him?

Impossible! Or was it?

He stepped to the window and, standing to one side,
peered out.

A crowd of people, both men and women, were coming
around the corner, coming toward his office. And in the
van was . . . was . . .

He stepped back from the window and felt his heart
begin to pound, with slow, heavy, impossibly loud beats.
That man walking ahead of the crowd was Clay Bell.
Alive . . . not dead.

Wheeling, with an almost animal grunt, he jerked open
a desk drawer, then another . . . another. . . . He had no
gun. He had left it in his room. He had left it at the
hotel.

The shock passed. He straightened and faced the door.
"Devitt!"

That was Bell, damn him! Bell, yelling to *him*!

He stepped quickly to the door and jerked it open.
The shock was gone but it had left something behind,
something he had never known before—a deep, burning,
driving lust to smash, to maim, to kill. . . .

"You wanted me?"

His voice was icy cold, yet his body was trembling.
There was the hated face, the man he wanted to destroy.

Clay Bell had never wanted to kill a man. He had never even wanted to fight a man. Yet, despite that, he had to admit in all honesty that once the battle was joined, he liked to fight.

Now, for the first time, remembering that Devitt had ordered the attack that had killed Bert Garry, that he had hired killers to shoot him, he found that he did want to fight. Jud Devitt was a man who only understood strength. Clay had handed over his guns with one idea in mind. He was going to meet Devitt on his own grounds, on his town terms.

Wat Williams had said what a fighting man Devitt was. All right . . .

The door burst open in response to his call and Jud Devitt stood there.

Clay felt a curious shock of surprise. The man was disheveled, almost dirty. But he was a big man, and in that moment, standing alone, Devitt showed that he was not afraid.

He was big, both taller and heavier than Clay, and the expression in his eyes was murderous. He started to speak, and then with a whining cry of inexpressible fury, he hurled himself from the door.

Clay stepped forward quickly to meet the attack, but even as he jerked up his hands, Devitt's body struck him, knocking him back and down. Devitt went down with him, and both men rolled over and scrambled to their feet. Devitt was fast—surprisingly fast. He landed on his feet and he swung. The blow caught Bell on the side of the face and staggered him, but he clinched quickly, back-heeled Devitt, and threw him to the ground.

He stepped back and Devitt came up in a lunging dive. As Clay stepped back, his boot turned on a stone and he fell, taking a wicked swing in the face. Both men got up and walked into each other, swinging with both hands. Devitt was coldly, wildly furious. This man had balked and defeated him, but now he was here, where he, Devitt, wanted him. Where he could smash and destroy.

He staggered Bell with a right, and lunged in, butting with his head. Clay raked his face with an elbow, and slammed a right to the body and then a left. Clay jabbed, then pushing Devitt off, shook him to his heels with an uppercut.

Devitt lunged, and his fingers caught Clay's shirt, ripping it down the front. He grabbed at Clay, and slugging wildly, they went to the ground. They rolled over and over, striking and gouging, and then broke free and scrambled to their feet.

Devitt threw a right, and Clay stiffened a left to his mouth that smashed his lips to a pulp. Instantly, Clay crossed a right to the chin. Devitt took it coming in and swung both hands with savage hatred.

But Devitt's cold fury was settling into shrewd, driving, fighting skill. He was a man who could fight and who liked to fight. He had never lost a rough-and-tumble battle, and had often boasted he could whip any lumberjack in his crews, and had often proved it.

He bored in, using his head. He punched hard to the body and was surprised to find the punch blocked. Those months in New Orleans with Jem Mace had taught Clay Bell more than a little. Now, fighting for his life, he realized the true value of all he had been taught by the aging bare-knuckle champion.

Clay jabbed a left, moved and jabbed again. Devitt landed hard to the body, and Clay gasped for breath, feeling the sickening force of that punch. Devitt struck him on the kidney and Clay's knees buckled. He clinched, swung hard to the ear, and felt the cartilage split under his fist. Then he smashed his right to the ribs and broke free. Devitt was streaming blood from the split ear and from his mouth.

Suddenly Devitt feinted, and Clay stepped in and caught a looping right that knocked him down. He rolled over, saw Devitt coming at him to kick, and then hurled himself at Devitt's legs. The bigger man sprang back and Clay started up. Devitt kicked out, the boot narrowly missing Clay's head but catching his shoulder and knocking him to his knees again.

Devitt rushed and Clay saw the boot swing back and

threw himself against the one standing leg. Devitt went down, and then they both got to their feet.

Clay hit him with a right, a bone-jarring blow that loosened teeth, then swung a right to the body. Devitt gasped and backed up. He tried to cover, but Clay pawed his hand away and struck him in the mouth. Devitt swung wildly, and Clay hit him on the chin.

Devitt bored in, swung a looping right and Clay saw lights burst in his brain. He tottered, and a fist smashed his jaw. He staggered, tried to clinch, but Devitt shook him off.

Devitt swung, and Clay grabbed the arm with both hands, flinging Devitt around and to the ground. Devitt came up and Clay threw a high hard one that caught Devitt on the chin. He went to his knees and Clay grabbed him by the shirt and jerked him erect, smashing his fist twice to Devitt's face and once into his body. The man's knees sagged and Clay flung him against the building, where he hit with a thud.

He staggered away, then fell flat . . . .

Swaying on his feet, unable to believe it was over, Clay Bell waited. A muscle twitched in Devitt's back, no more.

Bell turned, mopping blood and sweat from his face.

Hank Rooney jerked a thumb at the fallen man. "What'll we do with him?"

"Throw him on the night train, stuff his money in his pockets . . . get rid of him."

Clay Bell's head was throbbing. He walked to the water trough and ducked his head once, then again. He splashed water on his body, and somebody came running from the hotel with a fresh shirt. He dried himself, then pulled on the shirt.

The crowd stood around, unwilling to believe the savage afternoon was spent, but Clay Bell turned away and began to walk toward Tinker's. He wanted to get away, to stay away, to be back on his porch with evening coming on and the stars.

Colleen was waiting on the hotel porch and as he came up the steps she went to him quickly. Her eyes went to a gash on his cheekbone and she started to lift her fingers to touch his battered face.

He caught her wrist. "Your father inside?"

"Yes, but don't you think you should—"

He looked past her shoulder. "Sam, send somebody for that tall piano player from the Homestake. You can be best man."

"What about me?" Colleen put her hands on her hips. "Aren't you even going to ask me?"

"Never ask 'em," Clay tried to smile with his swollen lips. "Tell 'em!"

"Well—" Colleen hesitated.

"Inside," Clay told her, and held the door open.

Sam Tinker heaved himself to his feet. It was a good town, Tinkersville, a good place to live.

He looked down the street. It was almost empty of men. The crowd had drifted to the bars to talk of the fight. Down the street a cowhand leaning against an awning post struck a match on his chaps. Somewhere a door slammed, and from the corner of the Tinker House Sam looked off toward Deep Creek, beyond Piety, where those thousands of trees were still standing, breathing with the wind, shedding their needles, and where Deep Creek still ran clear and swift over its stones.

It was a good town, a good town. He would get the piano player himself.

ABOUT THE AUTHOR

LOUIS L'AMOUR, born Louis Dearborn L'Amour, is of French-Irish descent. Although Mr. L'Amour claims his writing began as a "spur-of-the-moment thing," prompted by friends who relished his verbal tales of the West, he comes by his talent honestly. A frontiersman by heritage (his grandfather was scalped by the Sioux), and a universal man by experience, Louis L'Amour lives the life of his fictional heroes. Since leaving his native Jamestown, North Dakota, at the age of fifteen, he's been a longshoreman, lumberjack, elephant handler, hay shocker, flume builder, fruit picker, and an officer on tank destroyers during World War II. And he's written four hundred short stories and over fifty books (including a volume of poetry).

Mr. L'Amour has lectured widely, traveled the West thoroughly, studied archaeology, compiled biographies of over one thousand Western gunfighters, and read prodigiously (his library holds more than two thousand volumes). And he's watched thirty-one of his westerns as movies. He's circled the world on a freighter, mined in the West, sailed a dhow on the Red Sea, been shipwrecked in the West Indies, stranded in the Mojave Desert. He's won fifty-one of fifty-nine fights as a professional boxer and pinch-hit for Dorothy Kilgallen when she was on vacation from her column. Since 1816, thirty-three members of his family have been writers. And, he says, "I could sit in the middle of Sunset Boulevard and write with my typewriter on my knees; temperamental I am not."

Mr. L'Amour is re-creating an 1865 Western town, christened Shalako, where the borders of Utah, Arizona, New Mexico, and Colorado meet. Historically authentic from whistle to well, it will be a live, operating town, as well as a movie location and tourist attraction.

Mr. L'Amour now lives in Los Angeles with his wife Kathy, who helps with the enormous amount of research he does for his books. Soon, Mr. L'Amour hopes, the children (Beau and Angelique) will be helping too.

"REACH FOR THE SKY!"

and you still won't find more excitement or more thrills than you get in Bantam's slam-bang, action-packed westerns! Here's a roundup of fast-reading stories by some of America's greatest western writers:

☐	THE PITCHFORK PATROL	Clay Fisher	8829—95¢
☐	APACHE	Will Comfort	8496—95¢
☐	SHALAKO	Louis L'Amour	8381—$1.25
☐	THE CROSSING	Clay Fisher	8337—95¢
☐	TROUBLE COUNTRY	Luke Short	6487—$1.25
☐	THE RIDER OF LOST CREEK	Louis L'Amour	2735—$1.25
☐	TREASURE MOUNTAIN	Louis L'Amour	2631—$1.25
☐	FEUD AT SINGLE SHOT	Luke Short	2618—$1.25
☐	CALLAGHEN	Louis L'Amour	2589—$1.25
☐	SACKETT	Louis L'Amour	2488—$1.25
☐	OVER ON THE DRY SIDE	Louis L'Amour	2452—$1.25
☐	DESERT CROSSING	Luke Short	2438—$1.25
☐	THE DESERTERS	Luke Short	2421—$1.25
☐	RADIGAN	Louis L'Amour	2339—$1.25
☐	RIDE THE DARK TRAIL	Louis L'Amour	2319—$1.25
☐	THE HIGH GRADERS	Louis L'Amour	2138—$1.25
☐	I, TOM HORN	Will Henry	2051—$1.50

Buy them at your local bookstore or use this handy coupon for ordering:

Bantam Books, Inc., Dept. BOW, 414 East Golf Road, Des Plaines, Ill. 60016

Please send me the books I have checked above. I am enclosing $_____
(please add 35¢ to cover postage and handling). Send check or money order
—no cash or C.O.D.'s please.

Mr/Mrs/Miss_____

Address_____

City_____State/Zip_____

BOW—2/77

Please allow three weeks for delivery. This offer expires 2/78.

BANTAM'S #1
ALL-TIME BESTSELLING AUTHOR
AMERICA'S FAVORITE WESTERN WRITER

- ☐ **HIGH LONESOME**   10450 $1.50
- ☐ **TREASURE MOUNTAIN**   10542 $1.50
- ☐ **SACKETT'S LAND**   10552 $1.50
- ☐ **THE FERGUSON RIFLE**   10618 $1.50
- ☐ **KILLOE**   10765 $1.50
- ☐ **CONAGHER**   10767 $1.50
- ☐ **NORTH TO THE RAILS**   10791 $1.50
- ☐ **THE MAN FROM SKIBBEREEN**   10798 $1.50
- ☐ **SILVER CANYON**   10822 $1.50
- ☐ **MOJAVE CROSSING**   10838 $1.50
- ☐ **REILLY'S LUCK**   10845 $1.50
- ☐ **GUNS OF THE TIMBERLAND**   10895 $1.50
- ☐ **HANGING WOMAN CREEK**   10896 $1.50
- ☐ **FALLON**   10897 $1.50
- ☐ **UNDER THE SWEETWATER RIM**   10901 $1.50
- ☐ **MATAGORDA**   10902 $1.50
- ☐ **DARK CANYON**   10905 $1.50
- ☐ **THE CALIFORNIOS**   10906 $1.50

**Buy them at your local bookstore or use this
handy coupon for ordering:**

Bantam Books, Inc., Dept. LL, 414 East Golf Road, Des Plaines, Ill. 60016

Please send me the books I have checked above. I am enclosing $_____
(please add 35¢ to cover postage and handling). Send check or money order
—no cash or C.O.D.'s please.

Mr/Mrs/Miss_____

Address_____

City_____State/Zip_____

LL—2/77

Please allow three weeks for delivery. This offer expires 2/78.

Bantam Book Catalog

It lists over a thousand money-saving best-sellers originally priced from $3.75 to $15.00 —bestsellers that are yours now for as little as 60¢ to $2.95!

The catalog gives you a great opportunity to build your own private library at huge savings!

So don't delay any longer—send us your name and address and 25¢ (to help defray postage and handling costs).